MUTUAL IN LOVE DIVINE

MUTUAL IN LOVE DIVINE

A Narrative

Pete Najarian

REGENT PRESS
Berkeley, California

{paperback}
ISBN 13: 978-1-58790-603-9
ISBN 10: 1-58790-603-1

{e-book}
ISBN 13: 978-1-58790-605-3
ISBN 10: 1-58790-605-8

Library of Congress Control Number: 2021029585

Printed in the U.S.A.

REGENT PRESS
Berkeley, California
www.regentpress.net

"Awake! awake O sleeper of the land of shadows, wake! expand!
I am in you and you in me, mutual in love divine."

From the opening of
William Blake's *Jerusalem*

For the families I lost in the
death march and the massacre.

The Minor Third   11

The Dead   17

The Candle   22

Vipassana   30

Song   39

Bresson's Donkey   47

The No Money Work   55

Yellow   64

To Norm   71

Dear Cathleen   83

Gregory   100

The I   110

Freud's Story   118

After the Massacre   130

To Ellen Pinsky   144

Armenia, 7 December 1988   153

Juju   167

Acknowledgments   168

The Minor Third

Musically illiterate and tone-deaf since birth, I learned from a feature on NPR's *To the Best of Our Knowledge*, "Why Do We Love Sad Songs?" that Samuel Barber's *Adagio for Strings* was written, like all sad music, in the minor third, though the twenty-six-year-old Barber was happily in love when he wrote it in Paris in 1936.

Then, after Toscanini commissioned it for orchestra, it was played all day when Franklin D. Roosevelt died, and it's been played at funerals ever since.

But there was no mention of Shostakovich's third movement of his Fifth Symphony that was an elegy for the victims of Stalin and was for me the most heartbreaking music of all.

The *Adagio* had overwhelmed me when I first heard it as a boy, though not until I learned from *To The Best of Our Knowlege* that the minor third in speech would be like "let go," did I realize I've been keening a minor third all my life.

My father had his stroke by the time Roosevelt died, and we had a radio on the little Frigidaire in the kitchen where my brother would listen to *Make Believe Ballroom*, and it may have been on that day when I first heard the *Adagio*, since it always seemed to echo from my ancient past.

"What's your saddest jazz song?" asked the NPR program host, and without pausing I said to my cat curled at my elbow: Louie Armstrong's *Black and Blue*, composed by Fats Waller: *"Even the mouse/ran from my house . . ."*

I never knew a minor from a major or a sharp from a flat, but I was a child prodigy in my love for music when my mother, who was earning "good money" with her piecework in the post-war boom, bought an RCA console so my father could "play records while he was home alone all day," though I couldn't imagine how when he was half paralyzed.

Then my brother Tom began buying Turkish-Armenian music, since like my father he too loved "oriental music," and Tom also bought the early Sinatras and Artie Shaws and all the others of the Forties that would, along with the bubbly oud and wild violin, become the folk music of my childhood.

But one day Tom brought home a twelve-inch album of another kind of music, and then another and another, and though he himself rarely listened to them, I would sneak into the albums when he wasn't home, why I don't know, maybe because it sounded heroic like the movie music in our little neighborhood theatre.

And so, by the time I was in third grade I knew by heart every one of those albums that I can now not only list, but even remember the colors of their hardbound covers:

Beethoven's Violin Concerto,
Brahms's Third Symphony,
Tchaikovsky's Violin Concerto and Fifth Symphony,
Rimsky-Korsakov's *Scheherazade*
Wagner's "Overture to *Tannhauser*,"
Bizet's *Carmen Suite Caucasian Sketches* by Ippolitov-Ivanov,
Lalo's *Symphonie Espagnole*,
and of course Khachaturian's Piano Concerto
and Violin Concerto and *Gayane* ballet suite.

I remember it was the third grade because my third-grade teacher, Miss Mandelkern, was talking about music, and when I told her my brother had a Khachaturian album, she who was so strict got so excited I brought it the next day so she would love me.

Yet how terrified I was that my brother would find out, since he was like Stalin to me then.

"Don't play with my records!" he had said in the same way he said not to touch anything of his.

Though only nineteen, my brother had become the tyrant of our little row of rooms where my father sat impotent and my mother was always working; yet it was Tom himself who became the patron of my prodigious love.

And so coming home on rainy afternoons, I would delve into his albums while my father sat silent in the corner, and stacking with my little fingers the precious records, so frightened they would break when they dropped with such a loud clap on the metal plate, I would enter that realm where praising myself in the parlor mirror I became the conductor of the universe.

Then standing on a stool and waving my mother's wooden ladle like a wand, I would rise and flow with all those magical crescendos and andantes, while who knew what my father, who sat so silent in the corner, might be thinking of his little boy to whom he couldn't speak and who couldn't speak to him, my father to whom I would be writing for the rest of my life, as if he were the very silence of the cosmos.

He must have also loved music, since my mother said he had taught himself the violin after he escaped to America, and during the boon of the 1920s he could even afford a violin and lessons for his little nephew Ashod who would become my cousin Archie.

His older brothers, my mother would say, were such good musicians before their necks were sliced that "the Pasha himself" had them sing and play the zither.

It was in those ancient times before the phonograph when everyone knew how to sing and play, since music was what made us human, though live music would vanish after my father's stroke, and only the records would be left.

And so the years passed until my father died and my brother married and moved away, and when the albums evolved to the 33s and the console converted into a cabinet, I would buy them with what I earned from my paper route to play on our new portable stereo.

Mussorgsky's *Pictures at an Exhibition* was one of them and I could actually see them in my mind's eye, since music had always been visual to me, and though I couldn't read the notes of sheet music, I could wave my wand as if painting landscapes like those in Disney's *Fantasia*, where I first heard *The Rite of Spring* and Beethoven's *Pastoral Symphony* In the meantime, in the noon-hour dance of my little high-school gym came the new rock 'n' roll, and I might have enjoyed its powerful rhythm, rooted as it was in the same jazz of my brother's bebop, had I not become by then so crippled by the fear of crossing the court for the girl of my longing where the knots of my sexual frustration tightened behind my eyes in the agony of the ages.

The new rock 'n' roll, so explosive and vital, was dance music, but I was too afraid to dance, and I still can't dance to this very day and never crossed the court and let go of my fear.

I was always afraid and I may have been born afraid. I was afraid of the dark, as in the darkness of the cellar where a dragon lay coiled under the boiler, and most of all I was afraid of being alone, though I would live alone for the rest of my life.

And yet something kept me alive as if it were in my very breath, and my private music seemed a part of it, like when I would later hitch across the continent so alone yet unafraid on the dark highway where I whistled my Scheherazade to the silence of the stars.

And so by the time I left for college my love for music was so much part of me it seemed connected to my need to write, as if it were the mother of all the arts and the breath of life itself, the *AUM* a Buddha would hum to the void until the silence would hug me like a father and I would never be afraid again.

Then at Rutgers in New Brunswick, in that first September when I moved into the freshman dorms, I walked to the student center one evening, and suddenly streaming from across the hall came what the disc jockey happened to play that night, and it pierced me as if I were a Percival struck by a vision of the Grail.

Yet it wouldn't be until a lifetime later that I learned from Michael Tilson Thomas' *Keeping Score*, that this music, which came from a cello and an oboe and a harp, was derived from a hymn in the Russian orthodox church that was like a hymn in the little Armenian Church where I would light a candle for my father to be whole again.

"Please make my father better," I would whisper over the candles, Sunday after Sunday from when I was five to when he died when I was ten and never prayed again.

But I wasn't of course thinking this as I stood transfixed in the student center that night. I never thought anything when I listened to music, since that's what music was about when you really listened: you stopped thinking and closed your eyes and saw a vision of an opening space in the rise and fall of your breath, as I did that night not knowing I was hearing the slow movement of Shostakovich's Fifth Symphony, composed not only for the victims of the Purge but the nightmare of history itself, since that's what music was also about, the wail and cry even wolves and whales will sing when they lose each other and search for home.

And so the weeks passed in that blaze of being eighteen when you throb with life and can't get enough of it, and one afternoon, returning from my outdoor P.E. class to the lockers in the gym, still in my red and black shorts and T-shirt, I came upon a music that was not really music but a cacophony of instruments the Philadelphia orchestra was tuning to rehearse for a concert that night.

And never having heard such instruments live before, I sat in one of the chairs that filled the gym, entranced by how beautifully the sounds flew and fluttered like birds whistling and chirping and competing with one another.

Then they stopped, and a little old white-haired man limped to the podium, and he was the great Eugene Ormandy who was lame and whose only audience was of course the kid in his gym shorts looking up again like a Percival in awe.

And then there was a pause.

Or maybe there wasn't and I'm imagining it all, yet what difference would it make, since I was that child again with his crippled father and his mother's wooden ladle, and the little old white-haired conductor struck his wand and cracked the silence with the opening of Brahms's First Symphony that was the greatest of all symphonies....

And I lay stunned as in my first wet dream when the cosmos opened and the light poured through, and the old cripple was now the lame god Hephaestus himself saying through Brahms that there would be no more elegies but only triumph and apocalypse, as in the triambos to Dionysus and the apokalupsis in the unveiling of the Grail.

"You're not a cripple," he said, "you never were a cripple, let go your fear and dance the dance of the ages, let go, let go!"

Photo by Tom when he was 12

The Dead

I had just turned seventeen, and my mother and I had moved to the lower half of a duplex that had a backyard with a grapevine where we sat one Sunday morning in October when the leaves were turning, and while she folded the laundry she had dried on the line, I opened the little Dell paperback I had bought from a rack in a drug store around the corner, *Six Great Short Novels,* in which the first was called *The Dead,* by a James Joyce I had never heard of.

I was only an average reader, but I was very sensitive to the music of English prose, and I was suddenly grabbed by the first sentence that began with "Lily, the caretaker's daughter," as if it were the opening of a song.

I didn't know then that the lily was a funeral flower, nor did I know what the story was really about, but the sentences flowed so beautifully I couldn't stop reading until the very end.

Later in college I read what T.S. Eliot once wrote about reading a poem first for its music and then its meaning, but I wouldn't really know the meaning of Joyce's early masterpiece until a lifetime later.

I moved away from my mother when I left for college, but as the years passed I was always in touch with her, and after she retired and moved to Fresno I would drive there from Berkeley and stay for the weekend.

One weekend I walked to a Long's Drugs near her home to rent a video we could watch in the evening after dinner, and it so happened that John Huston's film of *The Dead* was on the shelf.

I had seen it a few years earlier when it first came out in a theatre, and I was curious what my mother would think of it. Her English was good enough by then that she could enjoy the films I would rent, and I would enjoy her enjoyment of them.

She was an intelligent woman, but I didn't learn this until her old age when I could see her apart from being her son. She had been a peasant girl before the massacre, and after surviving the death march and coming to America, she worked in a factory for the next fifty years and yet never learned to read.

Her first language was Turkish and she didn't learn Armenian until the English brought Armenian teachers to her orphanage in the hills above Beirut after freeing it from the Turks, and she wanted to stay there and be schooled, but a wealthy Armenian family came saying they would adopt her, and they brought her down to the city and made her a servant instead.

She lived with them for two years and learned some Arabic in the streets when she would deliver her master's lunch to his office, and she would later use her Arabic in America when her first job was in a factory with Syrians, and in the meanwhile she spoke only Armenian with her first husband's family and didn't learn English until years later when she worked with Italians who spoke it with an accent.

So as the years passed she never learned to read and couldn't of course read me stories when I was a child, but she was a great storyteller and I would love to listen to her Armenian mixed with Turkish and Arabic and her broken English, and one of her stories was when she fell in love with my father when the young survivors had a theatre group in West Hoboken and he was a prompter in a hood on the stage where she had a small part as a housemaid like Lily in *The Dead*. Back in her home from Long's Drugs with Huston's film, I slipped it in the cassette player under her television and she relaxed in her rocking chair as I sat close by watching her enjoy it.

Huston was her age and he had made films for as long as she had worked in factories, and *The Dead* was his last that he directed in a wheelchair with an oxygen tank for his emphysema from his addiction to cigars, and he would die before it was released.

He was one of my favorite filmmakers and I had seen his masterpiece, *The Treasure of Sierra Madre*, when I was around eight and it played in a little movie theatre only a block from where I grew up.

He too loved Joyce whose language was supreme, but film had a different language and he had to translate from one to the other. I liked his film version when I first saw it, but it didn't move me like when I read it in the Dell paperback, and it wasn't until I watched it with my mother did I realize how supreme it was as well.

Joyce had written it around the time my mother and Huston were born, but it wouldn't be published until the war when my mother was on the march through Syria and Houston's own childhood was torn between his parents, and the confluence of their three lives flowed into each other as the film began and Lily the caretaker's daughter said to Gabriel, the protagonist, the same sentence as in the book:

"The men that is now is only all palaver and what they could get out of you."

My mother of course had no idea what this meant, and yet she was hooked by Lily's white apron and black dress that was the same as the one she wore in the Armenian play my father prompted when she too was a teen, and as Gabriel climbed the stairs from the pantry to the dinner party she followed him as if to all the dinners of her long life.

The dinners of her childhood were cooked over an outdoor fire when her family lived on their vineyard in Adana where it didn't rain from spring to autumn, and when they lived in a tenement room in the city during the rainy season, her mother would cook on a common stove in the yard, but even peasants had dinner parties with relatives, and they must have been like those I knew from my own childhood after my father died and she would cook for his relatives who had become her family as well.

She loved to cook and feed those she loved, and her eyes were glued to the screen as the camera scanned the faces around the table and Gabriel carved the goose.

She didn't of course know what the talk was about or its Irish politics in the mention of Parnell, but she knew what politics were like in its Armenian version when the Catholicos of all Armenians was stabbed to death in the Holy Cross church in Manhattan during the fight between the nationalists and the followers of the Soviet.

It was in the early years of the Depression, and after divorcing my brother's father she was a single mother for two years, and when my father split from his sister's family and lived in a rooming house they met in secret until they were finally able to marry.

She had turned thirty by then, and in the old photos in her closet her eyes were bright and her aquiline nose was like Huston's daughter Angelica's who played Gabriel's wife Gretta and like Gretta she too once danced to music, though it was not a quadrille with a piano but Turkish-Armenian songs with a bubbly oud and a wild violin and clarinet, the hardwood floors polished with beeswax and the winter coats piled on a bed like bodies without souls, the script by Huston's son Tony following faithfully Joyce's own cinematic genius as my mother watched intently like I once watched her perform for me when I was a toddler.

And then the party was ending and Gabriel looked up at Angelica's Gretta standing at the top of the stairs like my mother before I was born, their dark hair not the bronze of Joyce's Gretta and yet with the same visionary glow.

And now the music changed to a melancholy strain as Bartell D'Arcy sang *The Lass of Aughrim* that would lead to the death of the seventeen-year old Michael Furey, and I didn't pause the cassette to explain who he was while my mother was so caught by Angelica crying in her pillow with the nostril of her regal nose like her own when she once cried after my father was paralyzed by a stroke and she would tell me no stories until after he died.

"It was a good movie," she said in English after the last scene of the snow in the cemetery, "and now I'm going to bed."

She was only eighty then, and she had her own little grapevine in her yard in Fresno where it didn't rain from spring to autumn and she would tie the vines like her father in Adana, though not for the grapes but the delicate leaves for her *sarma* that she picked when they were young and tender and not tough with age like those sold in delicatessens.

She also had a wash-line in her yard, and she told my brother "no," she didn't want a drier since she loved to raise her arms and pin her wash on the line as if to praise the sky and her survival.

And I am back with her now when I was seventeen and reading *The Dead* while she folds her laundry that is redolent of the breeze no drier can match, and I too am in love with a girl like Gretta yet even more in love with writing, and I want to write like a James Joyce whose words are like music, not knowing I would still be writing my mother's story long after she was gone when I would be almost eighty myself.

The Candle

My brother died last week, and driving across the valley to his funeral I spoke to the sky as if it was listening.

I had been reading Sarah Rudin's new translation of Augustine's *Confessions* that she turned it into a kind of novel in which his narrator speaks to a "You" that she translates as his "master," and it reminded me of my own novels and my own master.

I was around five when my mother slipped a nickel in my palm to light a candle for my father who had been crippled by a stroke, and it was my brother who led me to the little Armenian church around the corner where he taught me how to drop the nickel in the brass box under the flames; then for the next five years I would pray as only a child can for a father I needed so desperately.

But who or what was I praying to as I stared over the candles at a little painting of a Jesus at the side of the altar, and what was the mystery behind the altar?

I was learning to read by then, but English was still new to me, and I would lip read in tasting each word instead of gobbling whole pages like my precocious friends.

Yet I loved my comic books, though more for their pictures than the words in the balloons, until there appeared in one of them a center section with only small print, and unable to read it, I followed the lines as if I could see a story it was supposed be telling.

And it was soon after that my mother brought my father and me to a relative's chicken farm in Freehold to escape the summer heat in the city, and it was like a happy dream with the chickens strutting like royalty even on the porch, and the tomato fields burst across the road with tomatoes as delicious as garden tomatoes when New Jersey was called "The Garden State" before agribusiness took the taste away.

There were no other kids around, but I was in a magical realm where there was no loneliness, and one evening when my mother was chatting in the parlor with old Dickran and Astkhig, the radio didn't work when I sat in the kitchen, and to entertain myself I wrote a story in the same way I imagined one in the center of the comics, though I couldn't write any better than I could read. Like all kids I loved stories, but I also needed to tell one, as if someone or something was listening.

My father died a year later, and though I didn't have to pray for him anymore, I continued to speak to what had vanished from beyond the candles to behind the sky and was maybe inside me as well?

The Korean War had started, and when my brother was sent abroad my illiterate mother made me write him letters, and it was in those letters that I first became the writer I am today. I had learned to read well enough by then that I could read the stories of Jack London in my cousin Archie's *Armed Services Edition,* and after reading Saroyan's *The Daring Young Man on The Flying Trapeze* in Archie's anthology by Somerset Maugham, I wanted to write just like it.

And so, I had become a writer and later went to college where one evening in Rutgers I started a story about my father that included Hemingway who was one of my father figures, and I would be writing this same story for the rest of my life: to be a man like who I had wanted my father to be, and now the question of who or what I was writing to became more urgent than ever.

I discovered poetry in Rutgers, thanks to my freshman class with Paul Fussell who assigned a paperback called *Sound and Sense,* and I was brought back to when I was first learning English and found that the music of words was tied to their sense, and the sense would resound in me as in the chant of AUM where what had gone from the candles to beyond the sky was inside me as well, and I would keep needing to find it.

Augustine had the same need, and Sarah Rudin as well. He loved the music of Latin, and she loved turning it into English.

"O Master, Master," he wrote in her English, "Who bent the sky downward and descended and touched the mountains and they smoked…." which came, said Rudin's footnote, from Paul's letter to the Galatians.

He constantly quotes Paul and the Psalms while speaking to the same You as his Master, but who or what was that You?

Was it the same as in Whitman's *Song of Myself* and Blake's *Prophecies* and Prospero's Epilogue and what Emily Dickinson couldn't *"see to see"* in her poem *I Heard a Fly Buzz When I Died.*

And was it the same as death, like the death of my brother as I drove across the valley with his ghost?

I didn't really get to know my brother until the last few years before he died. My first memory of him was when I was around three and he was teasing me by rubbing the new whiskers of his teens like sandpaper on my cheek as if he loved me.

But it was around the time of my father's stroke, and overwhelmed by the stroke, my mother would use him to discipline me, and I became afraid of him.

We lived in a small apartment of railroad rooms, and he would order me to stay away from his secretary desk, or carry the garbage pail to the cans in the cellar, or go buy the Sunday Mirror on the way to the bread from the Italian baker around the corner.

One day when I was playing in the street I scraped my knee so deeply he slapped my face to hold still while I squirmed away from the iodine, and his slap was telling me who was really boss in our home. We both looked like my mother and I never thought of him as my half-brother, but I would wonder if he felt the same about me.

On another day when I was sailing a raft of popsicle sticks in a gutter puddle, he walked by without saying a word as if he didn't know me. He worked in an ice-cream parlor in the afternoon, and when I bought a cone he took my nickel as if I were just another customer.

Yet he was so friendly with his Italian and Irish gang in their clubhouse and his Armenian gang in the meantime, and it was my fear of him that had turned him off. He didn't know how to relate to me and my fearful nature was opposite his, which my mother even pointed out.

Even when he was a baby she could take him anywhere and he would always be okay, but I would vomit from someone else's food. And when she took him to the barber for his first haircut, he sat happily on the board on the chair as if he were a prince; yet when she took me, she said, I was so frightened of the electric razor hanging from the ceiling that the barber couldn't control me and she had to take me to the barber across the street to finish the job.

He was good natured and never complained after she divorced his father when he was only four, yet there was something inside him he never talked about.

"Tommy feels everything," she said, "but he always holds it inside."

Nor did he ever talk with me except to tell me not to eat with my mouth open or not play with his records, and when he came home for dinner he would switch my radio programs to his *Make Believe Ballroom* without asking.

Yet one day around the time he taught me how to light a candle, he took me to the big fancy movie theater in Journal Square to see a western with Gary Cooper, and though he probably took me because my mother asked him to, it was one of the highlights of my childhood.

And when he wasn't home I would study the photographs of him with his gang as if he were my idol, and I wanted to be just like him. He was my big brother and I loved him like I loved my father, who also never talked with me since his lips were twisted by the stroke.

Like my father, who had been a jeweler, he was good with his hands and could write with either one, and when he and Archie came for a weekend at the chicken farm in his '36 Ford, I watched as they painted in the fields where he painted a beautiful landscape though he had never painted before.

He had a great eye and it was he who snapped the beautiful black and white photos when he was only twelve that I would later use in my book about my mother. He scored high in the Army I.Q. test, and they sent him to Germany instead of Korea and made him a photographer.

He was smart and talented, yet he didn't care. He didn't want to go college but to just be part of the gang and get a good job and have a family and be happy.

I was thirteen when he returned from the army, and having grown as tall as he I wasn't afraid of him anymore, and after he went back to his job as an apprentice in photoengraving, we would watch our new television in the evenings and go to the movies together. We still didn't talk, but I was happy being with him now, and one night we saw the new movie *Shane,* and it was like when he took me to see Gary Cooper in Journal Square.

But our new togetherness lasted only a year before he married and moved out, and I never saw him except with my mother when we visited, and if not for my mother I wouldn't have seen him again after I left for Rutgers.

He had banked on photoengraving when he finally got his union card, but photoengraving declined in the Sixties when he needed it the most to raise his kids, and after he moved to Fresno to start a new life my mother followed since they had always been inseparable.

Unlike me he had an optimistic nature and opened an Armenian delicatessen as if he could be part of an Armenian community like the one in Jersey, but Fresno was not like Jersey, and when the delicatessen went bust he had to start all over again, which was hard in his middle age.

"Your brother's not a business man," my mother said, "he's a worker like me."

Yet he persevered with one sales job after another until he could finally retire, and he was retired for about three years when we had to take our mother to a nursing home and his wife got cancer and his kids moved away, and he had a heart attack from all the stress.

But he recovered quickly, and after our mother and his wife and kids were gone, he lived alone, and I would drive down from Berkeley and stay the night, just as I had done with my mother.

He had a sharp memory and I would love interviewing him about the old days as if I were researching his biography. He knew my father better than I and had lived with him for ten years before the stroke. My father was actually more a father to him than he was to me, and I loved listening to his memories like the one when my father took him to the World's Fair in New York in 1939.

Then this past summer I made a special trip to see him after worrying about how many years he had left. My friends were dying one after another and I was thinking about death more than ever, and as I drove across the valley it was more beautiful than ever.

It was a wonderful visit and we went to A.J.'s Armenian restaurant on Maroa Street where the food was just like what our mother used to cook, and once again I interviewed him about the old days, and when we stood by my car as I was leaving I wanted to hug him.

But I didn't. No one hugged in our family except our mother. "I'll come again," I said.

"Maybe I'll drive up to Berkeley," he said. "I like Berkeley."

That was in August. I had wanted to drive down again but the weeks passed, and when he flew to Milwaukee to be with his son Tory for Thanksgiving, I worried after Tory's Facebook mentioned he wasn't feeling well.

But he called me as soon as he returned to Fresno. "I'm okay," he said. "Don't worry about me."

He had caught pneumonia on the plane to Milwaukee and was in the hospital there until he was well enough to fly back, and I stopped worrying when he sounded okay on the phone.

But a few days later Tory called from Milwaukee to say he was in the Fresno Kaiser Hospital. Tory flew there the following day, and after driving across the valley I met him in my brother's room in the intensive care unit.

The doctor had told Tory that the aneurysm was like "a ticking time bomb," and no one knew when it would explode. "It could be any minute or it could take a week or even two."

The aneurysm was in his chest and had spread to his kidney, and it may have begun years earlier when he had the heart attack. It had bothered him about four years before when he was offered a surgery with a fifty-fifty chance of survival that he declined with his usual optimism, but now it had caught up with him.

His mind was blurry and he was too weak to carry on a conversation, yet he was my same brother and even joked with the nurse's aide. Tory and I sat with him until evening and then went back to his house to sleep.

Tory would stay in Fresno and investigate a hospice if it was needed, but I didn't know what to do. I had nothing urgent in Berkeley, but I couldn't stay for weeks, so I decided to drive home in the morning and return a couple of days later.

He was still too weak to talk when Tory and I came in the morning, and I sat silent at his side while Tory was with the nurse at her desk. He looked just like my mother when she lay dying, but she was a hundred and he was only turning eighty-eight.

Then I stood up to leave, and I said,

"I have to go back to Berkeley now, Tom, but I'll come again in a few days."

But he knew his time was up, and he nodded for me to come closer to his face, and when I hunched to his face he pulled me to his cheek with tears in his eyes, and his whiskers were like when he cuddled me when I was a toddler, and I choked to keep from crying until I could make it to the elevator where I sobbed and fell apart.

He was still alive the next day, and Tory said over the phone that one of his fellow Shriners had come, and he even joked with him. But he was later in bad pain and needed morphine, and he died on his birthday the next morning, unconscious from the morphine.

The funeral wasn't until a week later, and Tory did the service since he's a pastor in the Metropolitan Church for the L.G.B.T. community that is a Protestant Christian denomination, and he quoted from the Bible like Augustine.

My brother wasn't a believer, but he had gone along with it to be part of the gang, and even my mother had gone along with it, though she wasn't a believer either. Once when we talked about what she really believed in, he said:

"The world was her cathedral."

But the only Bible I knew was from Blake and Rembrandt and Bach et al, a book of stories and poems in different forms and versions.

One day around forty years ago I was walking in the neighborhood of Cannaregio in Venice, and I stepped from the crowd into the little church of San Giovanni Grisostomo whose Greek Orthodox interior was like the little Armenian Orthodox church where I once lit a candle for my father, and as I looked at the Bellini painting of Saint Christopher, a middle aged woman came in from the street and dropped a coin in the box next to mine, and after lighting a candle she prayed to a painting of a Madonna as we each looked up with our separate faiths, mine in art and hers in her God.

It was late afternoon and she seemed as if coming from work she wanted to pray before going home to cook for her family, and her devotion was as if she were teaching me a gratitude for what gives us life.

Then in the Armenian monastery on the island of San Lazzaro, a young priest showed me the room where Byron read Armenian manuscripts, and in the room were a Buddhist text in Pali and an Egyptian mummy whose skin was like black leather, and the young priest had blond hair and blue eyes and said in Armenian that he was born in Hungary and his mother was Hungarian.

Then the next morning in the little flat where I was staying with young Tito and Antonio, their little radio reported the death of Sartre, who was an atheist.

And here now I am back in the farmhouse in Freehold while my mother is chatting in the parlor with Dickran and Astkhig and my father is sitting silent beside them, and I am in the kitchen writing my first story with the window open to the warm night and the rhythm of the crickets is weaving my lines like the hum of AUM resounding beyond the candle I once lit for my father to be well again.

Who are you to whom all writers write, O life, O death?

Vipassana

And what is death?

— It is the change in the living process of a particular body. Integration ends and disintegration sets in.

— But what about the knower? With the disappearance of the body does the knower disappear?

— Just as the knower of the body appears at birth, so they disappear at death.

— And nothing remains?

— Life remains. Consciousness needs a vehicle and instrument for its manifestation. When life produces another body, another knower comes into being.

— Is there a causal link between the successive body knowers or body minds?

— Yes, there is something that may be called the memory body, or causal body, a record of all that was thought, wanted and done. It is like a cloud of images held together.

— What is this sense of separate existence?

— It is a reflection in a separate body of the one reality. In this reflection the limited and the unlimited are confused and taken to be the same. To undo this confusion is the purpose of yoga.

The above is from *I Am That,* a book of talks with Nisargadatta, recorded and translated by Maurice Frydman in 1972 and sold at the time only at his house near Bombay, a humble home above a small shop his son ran after he retired.

My friend Babbo bought it there some years later and it caught my eye on his couch when he returned.

"You know," he said, "I was asked by a friend to buy a copy, and when I started reading it on the plane I smacked my head realizing I had just seen the teacher I had been looking for who I would never see again!"

In fact, I had been in Bombay myself when I too had never heard of him, and when I went to Shambala Books in Berkeley the clerk said:

"You know, we never had that book, it's not published in the States, but someone came in with a used copy just the other day!"

And I still have it by my bed, Babbo gone now seventeen years and I the same age as when he said over the phone as he lay dying:

"You can't expect to live longer than eighty, it's when everyone starts dying."

He was seventeen years older than I and I had always looked up to him while he never looked down to me, and I loved him like a wise uncle.

His name was actually Bill but his daughters called him Babbo that was Dad in Italian when they were first learning to speak, and he would be Babbo for the rest of his life except to friends from his youth.

He was born in 1923 and grew up so poor his mother had to leave him in foster homes, but she did love him and though life was hard for little Billy he would have happy memories of growing up by the sea in San Diego and his youth was filled with adventures until he enlisted when Pearl Harbor was bombed, and though his poor eyesight kept him in the States, he would later use the G.I. Bill in Italy to write his novel about his life in the Yukon and teaching in a one room backwoods schoolhouse, and when he couldn't get it published he and his sweet Jane took their kids to the Canary Islands where he was a headmaster of a grade school and a farmer and a businessman while the talented Jane helped pay the bills with her commercial art.

He never had a stable home as a child yet he would always provide a good life for his daughters, and when his ventures didn't pan out in the Canaries, he brought them back to the States and the farming he had always loved, and though that too didn't succeed they grew up happy and healthy until they were on their own.

He was turning fifty by then and Jane had re-married, and he was recovering from a liver disease that almost killed him when he had joined a group with Claudio Naranjo in Berkeley that I too would join when in spring 1973 Claudio imported a former monk from Thailand named Dhiravamsa who would teach vipassana meditation to about twenty of us in a ten-day retreat in the Sierra foothills.

It was at the spring equinox in an old Girl Scout summer camp rented during the winter where we slept in cabins, and after Dhira clanged us awake in the pre-dawn he explained in the meeting room that all we had to do was watch the rise and fall of our breath while keeping our backs straight without moving.

Babbo, who was very limber, could sit cross-legged, but the pain in my knees was so bad I had to ride a pile of pillows as if they were a horse like I did as a child, and with the ting of Dhira's little bell I watched my breath as it streamed from my navel to my head while the longer we sat the deeper it flowed into a stillness and calm.

We sat for about an hour until the ting for us to stop, and then as we followed Dhira through the woods he taught us how to watch the rise and fall of our steps where the stillness and calm was now in our walking, and after a light breakfast of tea and cereal we sat and walked again until lunch and then again until a light supper and his talk about the awareness and insight we might gain by our practice. He used the English word *meditation* that was about the mind, yet there was no word for what was happening inside me that was beyond thought and was tied instead to the streaming.

We would sit and walk for the next nine days and addicted to how good it felt I would continue on my own until Dhira returned the following year, and when he increased our sitting to two hours I felt the stream flow into my head as if it wanted to push through a hole in my skull like babies are said to have as if to expand, and I would continue to watch as it kept pushing.

Then in the third year it was suddenly like an electric charge through my shoulder and arm that made them spasm, yet there was no pain, and fascinated by its power I kept watching as it increased.

Meanwhile a few others were charged in others ways as if there were a current between us when Judy suddenly crooned and John erupted in shouts and Michael fled outside, and though Babbo, who I had yet to know well, sat quietly, and he would later tell me that the movement had been deep inside him since the first retreat.

I would never learn why some could sit quietly and others like me were different, yet we continued to sit for the rest of the day when I felt so electrified I couldn't eat at lunch or supper though I was usually a glutton, and the next morning my spasms were so powerful they would bump into what was her name on the next pillow and I had to sit alone in the back room where they spread to the rest of my body and were so wild I felt like the Biblical Jacob wrestling with an Angel, until afraid they were a kind of epilepsy I forced myself to tip-toe to Dhira and whisper I couldn't control them, so he came back with me and his presence helped me let them throw me around the room until I collapsed, and he returned to the group to ting the break for lunch.

I hadn't eaten since the day before nor wanted to now, and as I lay on the carpet the spasms were gone like the end of a storm and there was only the stillness and calm that was deeper than ever until I could rise and walk outside, and as I stood by the chickens the caretaker had left to peck in the grass I could feel in their bobbing and pecking the same peaceful waves inside me as if I were in a kind of Eden.

Who was I now inside my breath? And wanting more of it, I returned to my seat in the main sitting room where the rainbow colors of the soft light glowed like a chapel on the empty pillows and blankets in the rays of the sun through the window while the others were at lunch. I had been such a troubled and unhappy person most of my life and all I wanted now was to stay in the stillness by myself.

But who was that coming up the steps to sit and write in her journal? Oh well, I would stay in my breath and ignore her, and yet the scratch of her pen was like the buzz of a fly as if to torture me. She was at least thirty feet away yet I could hear the scratch as if it were chewing through my cochlea until I wanted to strangle her to make her stop. Scratch, scratch, she kept scratching as if she were burrowing into all the hatred of my life until it suddenly exploded into a scream that ripped apart every fiber of my being like an atomic blast, and I sat stunned as if I were electrocuted.

And then came the deep sobbing as if with an endless grief and a wrenching guilt, yet for whom or for what? I tried to think of my mother and father but it was deeper than anywhere I could remember or conceive.

Exhausted and empty, I rested until the group came with Dhira to begin the afternoon sitting, and as I returned to my breath I felt it stream through me with a new movement like a deep yawn that would expand in our walking like the moves of Tai Chi and the asanas of yoga.

It was called *chi* or *kriya* or *shakti* or *kundalini,* or what Blake called *energy* and Reich *orgone* and Whitman *the body electric,* or what science called *the spontaneous movements of the autonomic nervous system,* yet these were only words and I would follow it for the rest of my life.

And so, the years would pass as it developed inside me and Dhira would say to stay with it since it was in him as well, which I would witness when sitting beside him one day I watched him settle into his posture and let it stream through him so smoothly he could sit as long as when he was a monk who once sat from dawn to dusk.

"You're very fortunate," he said when it began to stretch inside my navel and make me belch and hyperventilate and have to sit alone so not to disturb anyone, and it would keep stretching as I kept sitting with him until he stopped coming to California and I couldn't follow him abroad.

Yes, I was fortunate in how it would cure me of the painful headaches I would never have again and the belching and exhaling would leave me immune to the dyspepsia so common in others, yet as it healed my body it would always remain separate from my troubled mind that I would talk about with Babbo when we became friends.

Neither of us stayed with Claudio after the third retreat though we continued to sit with Dhira, and after his daughter Reny moved to Australia he lived with her sister Taly who married Charles, a wealthy biochemist who retired at forty to settle in a vineyard in the Sierra Nevada where Babbo would share with him his expertise in viticulture.

It was by Camptonville near Nevada City and had been abandoned for years until Charles remodeled the old farmhouse and built another, and one weekend when I drove up from Berkeley to visit, Babbo and I hiked into the woods to a creek of the Yuba River where we sat naked on a boulder by a pool and talked as always about what was happening inside us.

His movements were as powerful as mine with his own version of the primal scream and the sobbing and the beneficial stretching, while he too had his own slough of despond in which he would sink to when his mother abandoned him as a child.

I loved hearing about his life however hard it was, especially his childhood when moving from home to home he would plant seeds in the different yards and return to see them grow. He loved plants and was a born farmer despite "going under' after "an early freeze" or when "the bottom fell out of the market" that made him flee "leaving debts behind." Now thanks to Taly's love for him and Charles' money, he could indulge his passion and even earn some extra cash selling his flowers in town.

Life had worked out for him and his biography was the opposite of mine in how he raised a family and always lived with a woman who was now Cecilia back at the farmhouse, yet as we sat on the boulder by the beautiful pool we were both on the same path of watching our breath and where it would lead. Then suddenly out of the woods appeared a pair of pubescent girls prancing naked with budding breasts and hairless pudenda as innocent and natural as fawns. They were the granddaughters of the counter-culture that had fled the city in search of a new Eden after Eve and Adam were banned in the old one where she hid her mons and he his eyes in shame, and now it was shame that would be banned as the girls spotted the two old geezers on the boulder and then hopped into the forest like fairies immune to lust.

Back at the farmhouse Babbo, who was a fabulous cook, began preparing the sea bass he had asked me to bring from Berkeley while Taly and Cecilia helped with the side dishes.

He had an affair with Cecilia when he was fifty and she in her twenties, and he didn't see her again until she appeared with her little Sol who Babbo would virtually adopt, which would work out perfect since Sol was the same age as Taly's and Charles' little Kayle and the two boys would grow up like brothers.

And so, we all gathered like one big happy family around the long table in the spacious kitchen cum living room with the sea bass smothered in Babbo's delicious sauce and the sprinkles of fresh cilantro and scallions from the garden.

He had worked hard all his life for the togetherness he would now share with me and then send me back to Berkeley loaded with his fresh corn and tomatoes and some brown eggs from his chickens. And in the meantime, he would keep sitting with his movements.

"I give them two hours every morning," he said, "but they always want more."

They were different from mine and yet came from the same place and he had been sitting with them for more than twenty years when his life that had seemed so idyllic began to change when Taly and Charles were breaking up after she visited her sister in Australia and fell in love with an Australian. In the meantime, Babbo, now close to eighty and unable to perform in bed with Ceciia, stepped aside while she coupled with Charles, and both families were to move to Australia when his liver disease returned, which was when I called him in the hospital in Sacramento and he said everyone starts dying at eighty. A mutual friend later told me Cecilia said he died peacefully as if he had finally seen the light he had been searching for all his life. If so, he must have been beyond Babbo by then, since the light, if it did exist, was beyond being seen as he himself once said about the ego: "The 'I' cannot be enlightened."

That was seventeen years ago, and turning eighty I would think of him every time I watched my breath, though I no longer gave it two hours in the morning but only an hour in the afternoon or half an hour or none at all. I began to have in my thirties what was called *segmented sleep* where I would wake in the middle of the night and then get up to breathe and stretch, but I grew lazy in my old age and would stay in bed to read when lo and behold my breath would begin the belching and exhaling on its own like an old friend.

It was my life and I wanted to hold on to it, yet once, when I was so sick and dizzy with the flu it couldn't stream inside me, I was reminded that it would help me while I was alive but would have nothing to do with my death, nor did I know what death really was. It was everywhere and always with the memories of my father dying in a charity ward and my mother in a nursing home and my dying brother and my friends and the touch of the cold and dusty arm of the Armenian girl I uncovered in the rubble of the earthquake and of hugging my dog as the vet slipped the needle in her paw and I couldn't stop sobbing the old sobbing from somewhere deeper than memory until he carried her away and later mailed me her cremains, and yet I was still alive and I went back to my breathing.

It was my yoga that Nisargadatta said would undo the confusion of my troubled mind, and I would watch it stretch my spine and noodle the muscles in my shoulders and make me belch and exhale, yet as Babbo had said it would keep wanting more as if I should do nothing else until it unraveled all the knots that had woven my life of always striving and craving, and I didn't want to do nothing else, I wanted to hold on to my life however troubled and unhappy it was, and I would give it only those hours when it would make me feel refreshed and full of energy, and then like Babbo I would return to my writing like he would to his garden before he died in the hospital. For writing was my other yoga and had been since I was a boy of nine in love with stories and needed

to write one of my own, from way back in that summer when my mother brought my father and me to a relative's chicken farm to escape the heat in the city, and staying in the kitchen while they sat in the parlor one night, I imitated the stories I loved in the radio and the movies and the comic books, and though I would forget what my own was about I would always remember the need to tell it, if for no one but myself and the hum of the crickets through the screen of the open windows with my lines in their same rhythm and the rise and fall of my breath I would keep breathing for the rest of my life until my I would disappear like Babbo and everyone else in the great cloud of the one reality.

Song

Sally Rooney's *Conversations with Friends* was so good I read it twice before I had to return it to the library's waiting list where it was already famous. It had the same fame as Hemingway's *The Sun Also Rises* that was said to be about his generation like her book about hers, and I was struck by how much more they had in common.

Both were in their twenties with a narrator telling a story about friends on vacation in southern Europe while each had a sexual wound, his from the battlefield and hers from endometriosis, and though they were as opposite as yin and yang, they were in the same sphere of storytelling with a special voice that made me want to write about them.

I was fourteen when I fell in love with Hemingway's voice in his story called *In Another Country* where his first sentence was *In the fall the war was always there, but we did not go to it anymore,* and though I was too young to notice the rhyme of *war* and *more,* it was like a music I was not aware of until then, and I found in the library his other stories and bought a little drugstore paperback of *For Whom the Bell Tolls* that all had the same rhythm I would imitate like a child following a father to this very day when I am old enough to have been his own father who was only 61 when he killed himself.

He killed himself in the summer of 1961 when I was turning twenty-one and started a story about him and my father as if they were friends. He was born in 1899 and my father in 1893, and they shared the same century as if…as if what, what was my story really about?

I had by then read all his work except what he didn't want published while he was alive, since unlike Thomas Wolfe, who was another of my father figures and the same age, he was his own editor and honed his lines as if they were poems I would read with the same love as for metered verse, as in the opening of his story *Now I Lay Me:*

That night we lay on the floor in the room and I listened to the silkworms eating. The silk worms fed in racks of mulberry leaves

*and all night you could hear them eating and a dropping sound in
the leaves. I myself did not want to sleep because I had been living
for a long time with the knowledge that if I ever shut my eyes in
the dark and let myself go, my soul would go out of my body. I had
been that way for a long time, ever since I had been blown up at
night and felt it go out of me and then come back. I tried never to
think about it, but it had started to go since, in the nights, just at
the moment of going off to sleep, and I could only stop it by a very
great effort. So while now I am fairly sure that it would not really
have gone out, yet then, that summer, I was unwilling to make the
experiment.*

I read these lines again when he shot himself. I was working
as a shipping clerk in the basement of the Rutgers University Press
that was in an old clapboard house where the office of the director
William Sloane was in the attic, and one day he came down to the
basement for some reason and stopped to chat with my foreman
Norm Fruchter and me and he told us of when he was a young
editor in the Twenties and a writer brought a manuscript that was
"Four feet high!

"So I grabbed a handful to read," he said, "and it was powerful, but I couldn't see myself editing four feet of it, and he took
it across the street to Charles Scribner's where Maxwell Perkins
turned it into *Look Homeward, Angel.*"

Hemingway also wrote stacks of pages four feet high, and
about eight hundred of them were in a manuscript he titled *The
Garden of Eden* that he began in 1946 and worked on until his
suicide, but only a small part was published after his death, and
though it was not of his best work it had the start of a story I
would save about a son and his father and the killing of an old
elephant.

Most of the chapters were about the main character and his
wife and a younger woman who slept with each of them, and the
androgyny led me to Hemingway's mother dressing him as a girl
and how his super masculinity was the other half of his feminine
tenderness. It's not easy to be a man, he wrote somewhere I can't
find now, and his sexual ambivalence surfaced painfully when one
of his sons, a super macho like himself, became a transsexual with

whom he fought so bitterly they never spoke again in the more than ten years he was writing *The Garden of Eden,* which might have been his most important work were he not so sick by then.

He loved his son and his son loved him like he loved his own father who had killed himself and who was like the father in *The Garden of Eden* when the son was eight years old and the old elephant was like a vision, and when the father shot the elephant the boy's guilt was as if he had betrayed his vision while the writing of the story was part of the plot except it was unfinished and the eight hundred pages would never be truly edited and the old elephant was all the animals he loved and killed when the photos of him holding the horns of a great buffalo and rhino were scattered at his shrine with the shotgun that shattered his own skull.

He loved animals like he loved life and he killed them in the same ambivalence as in the word Freud had coined with the Latin *valentia* from *valere,* "to be strong" that was the other side of the coin in Freud's life against death in *Civilization and Its Discontent.* All of Hemingway's writing was about life against death and yet his writing was his salvation until he could write no more and held the barrels of his shotgun in his mouth.

Or maybe it was because he inherited suicide? "How can anyone kill himself," my mother once said, "when their soul is so sweet?" But she used the Armenian word *seerd* for heart and not *hokee* for soul, and the difference in my mistranslation was like the lines of the silkworms eating when his soul went out of his body, though it was not his soul but his self and suicide was the killing of the self and no one knows if there is a soul or not, as in one of his greatest stories that was really a poem called *A Clean, Well-Lighted Place* about an old man who failed to hang himself and a waiter's dialogue of a self and a soul that didn't exist:

What did he fear? It was not fear or dread. It was a nothing that he knew too well. It was all a nothing and man was nothing too. It was only that and light was all it needed and a certain cleanness and order. Some lived in it and never felt it but he knew it all was nada y pues nada y nada y pues nada. Our nada who art

*in nada , nada be thy name thy kingdom nada thy will be nada
and nada our nada as we nada our nadas and nada us not into
nada but deliver us from nada; pues nada. Hail nothing full of
nothing, nothing is with thee.*

And yet he was a romantic writer who wrote beautiful
romances about heroes in love with young women and sang
of courage and *le coeur,* the heart, until his sickness overcame
him and he could sing no more. He needed to be strong and
was strong until he was crippled by his sickness that was not
only from alcohol but what had haunted him since his mother
dressed him as a girl when he fought so hard to be a man while
deep inside him was an eternal boy, or am I writing now as an
old man pushing myself up the trail of my own eight hundred
pages like a Sisyphus who keeps failing to find his soul as if it
were a girl in in a white rose of paradise?

I imagined Sally Rooney as the girl of my soul when I fell in
love with her writing, not the young author in the YouTubes of
her interviews, but the granddaughter I never had, as in *Anabasis*
by St. John Perse translated by T.S. Eliot:

*"Mon Ame, grand fille, vous aviez vos facons que ne sont pas les
notres. My soul, great girl, you had your ways which are not ours."*

She too was a romantic writer whose persona was in love
with her lesbian girlfriend and her married boyfriend while she
endured her menstrual disorder and wrote a story that was part
of the plot like Hemingway's elephant was part of *The Garden of
Eden;* then in her second book *Normal People* that was as good as
her first, she left her bisexual theme and wrote in the third person, and yet her romance continued with the young lovers like
brother and sister and the writing of a story was again part of the
plot, and it was her genius for plot and dialogue that she had in
common with Hemingway though their lives were the opposite.

His books were ignored by some women in the women's
movement because of his macho image, and in a YouTube interview she said she too was a feminist, but all genius in art is
androgynous.

Love genius, said Blake, *it is the face of God,* which meant
the same as Van Gogh saying he could do without God in his life

but not the power to create, which was how I became a writer after my father died when there was no need to pray for him anymore, though my writing would be like a prayer over the candles to the void behind the alter, until here now with Sally Rooney like the girl of the soul I lost and Hemingway my father figure whose sickness was unto death.

She too wanted to believe in the soul when her persona read the Gospel of St. Mark, but she couldn't except in the same genius of Blake's *Prophecies* and Van Gogh's devotion to paint. To create a plot with a dialogue or a pattern in a vanishing point was finding the girl Psyche who married the God of Love and became eternal, like when I drew a freshman boy while I was subbing in a high school in East Oakland.

He was sitting quietly near my desk watching the others run amok on the other side of the room, though he kept moving the angle of his profile and I had to wait for him to pause before I could catch how his cupid's bow curved into his philtrum as beautiful as a girl's as if I were kissing a joy as it flew into the point of eternity that would vanish with the bell.

It was a beautiful drawing that my power to create had made with my life of drawing lines like an old Ingres had said to a young Degas, *"Draw lines, my boy, keep drawing lines,"* and I asked the boy if he wanted it.

"Yes," he said, "I want to give it to my mother."

He loved his mother who was devoted to him, and he would love her until long after she was gone in his old age, yet there was no girl in my drawings who wanted to give one to a father, and wondering about a girl's love for a father I thought of my mother who lost her father when she was the same age as when I lost mine.

It was when they had come to Damascus that she called *Sham* in Turkish where he buried her baby brother by a church who had been born on the march and he too would be buried there. He was a church going man who she remembered taking her to church when they left their vineyard and moved to Adana during the winter rains and she said it was fitting that he was buried by a church.

She had told me only that he got sick and died and I didn't learn what sick meant until the end of her life when I was changing her diaper after her thighs were smeared with diarrhea as she looked up at me through her knees and said: "This was how my father died."

It must have been from a disease like typhus when he tried to flee to Aleppo that she called *Haleb* where he had relatives and they were forced from the train into the death march where her mother gave birth on the road, and after the baby and her father were buried in *Sham,* she and her mother and older brother were prodded toward Jerusalem until a Turkish soldier put her on a train with other children to the hills above Beirut and she never saw her mother and brother again.

But what I would ask did she eat in those six months on the road, and all she would say was weeds as if she didn't want to remember, and it would all blur in the death march of history and the anabasis of civilization where *Haleb* and *Sham* would be bombed into rubble in the Syrian civil war like the Spanish civil war in Hemingway's dispatch that was his most moving poesy, *Old Man at the Bridge,* where the old man worried about what would happen to the animals he had to leave behind. *"I was taking care of animals," he said. "I was only taking care of animals."*

There would always be what was left behind with wars and poesy, and in the meantime a young Sally Rooney would keep writing like the girl of my soul that was my need to finish my mother's story after her mother and brother disappeared into the bones in desert, and she too would be only skin and bones when the nurse's aide found she had died in the middle of the night, and when my brother called to tell me I remembered her memory of the petals of the mulberry blossoms falling on her face as she woke.

It didn't rain in the vineyard from spring to autumn and they slept in the open on a deck where I imagined their donkey slept under them, or maybe the donkey really did sleep there, but she was gone and I couldn't ask her anymore, nor had I ever seen a mulberry tree or knew if it had any silkworms eating with a dropping sound in the leaves or if she had a soul or not. Yet my mother's childhood in the vineyard was my Garden of Eden where her memories would blossom into the story I would be writing for the rest of my life.

"Tell us a story," said one of the kids where I was subbing last week.

"You tell me a story," I said. "Tell me about your grandmother who was my age."

She didn't know her, she said. Her mother was a baby when they fled from the massacre by Pol Pot in Cambodia, and in the class were the others whose grandparents fled from the massacres in El Salvador and Somalia and all the gardens left behind like Massacio's mural in the Brancacci Chapel of Eve and Adam leaving Eden with her arm hiding her breasts and his face buried in his hands, the brushstrokes in the fresco like lines of poesy that would turn the horror into a song with Massacio dying at twenty-seven and becoming the father of Michelangelo who continued the story in the mural of *The Last Judgement* in the Sistine Chapel where souls would climb from hell to heaven too high to see looking up from behind the altar.

My mother remembered her older brother drew pictures for the church when they lived in town during the winter. He was always drawing, she said, even in the vineyard, but she couldn't remember his face that had always been a blur after he was left behind on the march, until one morning when I was writing on her kitchen table she came in from her bedroom and said:

"I dreamt of my brother, my son, and I saw his face!"

It had been a blur for eighty years but now in the dream was suddenly as clear as a vision.

"What did he look like?" I said.

"How can I tell you?" she said. And he disappeared again in the anabasis to the desert, my little uncle who was like Massacio and Michelangelo.

Maybe he didn't die after he was left behind. Maybe an Arab saved him and made him a slave while she went to America where he came to her in a dream like Blake's vision of *Jerusalem* who was the feminine half of the masculine Albion in the Eden of eternity, maybe my little uncle was my imagination incarnate.

The Arab could have been a nomad who dragged him across the desert and saw him one day drawing with a pebble on a rock and sold him and the rock to a peddler who could have taken him beyond the desert to where I couldn't imagine his survival anymore and my mother never dreamt of him again.

One day in the year before she died I watched her looking out the window of her room in the nursing home as I sat at her side drawing her face. There were three beds in the room and her bed had been by the door until I asked to have her moved by the window after what was her name had died, more for myself than her who was beyond caring where she lay while her mind was slowly sailing over the years like a mission to outer space whose beeps grew fainter and fainter.

And yet she could still be coherent, and as she looked out the window the blossoms of the little plum tree were dropping their petals in the breeze and she asked in Armenian with the Armenian word *karun,* "Is it spring?"

And my pencil followed the wrinkles of her eyes as if I were tracing the map of her life from when she woke under the mulberry blossoms dropping their petals on her face to her survival across the century.

"I have to go now, Ma?" I said. "Where?" she said. "To your house," I said. "My house?" she said. "Can you remember your house?" I said.

But it was like a dream and the nurse had come to pull the curtain around the bed to change her diaper.

Outside the red sky was turning into the purples of the sundown, and after sleeping in the little house she had bought with her life savings, I drove across the valley leaving her behind.

Bresson's Donkey

One morning in the fall of 1966, I came to the Education Department of the British Film Institute on Old Compton Street in Soho where the late Peter Harcourt had ordered a film and asked if I wanted to watch it with him. Of course, I said, since I looked up to him who at thirty-five was nine years older than I and one of its brilliant lecturers.

I was new at the BFI where I was a teaching intern, though I was really a student myself and even the word *film* was new to me that was only the *movies* when starting at the age of five I would go with the neighborhood gang to the local movie house to watch for only a nickel the westerns and thrillers of the post war Forties, and when television appeared in the Fifties they would be played all day and night with the oldies of the Thirties and I would stay up late for them.

I loved them that were my first art, though I wouldn't think of them as art until I moved to London where what seems now like destiny I was led by friends to the BFI. I was in love with art since I was a kid, and to find my early love of cinema in the same realm as Rembrandt and Cezanne was monumental to me.

And so, I sat with Peter in the small viewing room where one of the lovely secretaries, what was her name, brought us tea and biscuits, and young Ian the projectionist took Peter's film out of the can to his booth behind us.

It was a recent French film called *Au Hasard Balthazar* by Robert Bresson who was just a name to me then, and it began with the birth of a donkey when before I knew what was happening it suddenly grabbed me like a trance and didn't let go until the end that was one of the most powerful I had ever seen.

And yet I had no idea what it was about, and still stunned I turned to Peter and said, "What was that about, Peter?" But he just smiled and said he would have to think about it.

Then out on Old Compton Street the world appeared as if washed by a vision that was how I always felt after seeing a work of art that would open my eyes with the opening of my heart.

What was it in the donkey Balthazar' eyes that was like an

illumination all art wanted to attain? One of the most moving moments for me in the film was when he looked into the eyes of the tiger and then the chimp and the elephant in the cages of a circus where he too was captive in our human realm, and it would later reverberate in the visionary scene where a flock of sheep would gather around him as he lay dying.

There was a story in the film about the human realm that was caught in its own chains, yet not as a drama in a theatre with actors, but with non-actors in a kind of mystery play where the donkey was the protagonist. Acting had become a major part of a cinema where the persona of the actor was dominant, but this was a new kind of film I had never seen where the donkey had no persona and could view the world free of the ego while the cast moved around him as if in a rite where the slash of the whip hitting him had a rhythm as striking as any score. I would later see Bresson's other films made in the same way, yet none would have the power of the donkey who was his ideal character for the kind of vision he wanted.

But what was that vision and how could I discuss it with a film study group?

Then one day when visiting the National Gallery that was only a short walk from Soho where I would go as often as I could, I was looking at Piero della Francesca's *Baptism of Christ* that was one my favorite paintings where the dove of the Holy Ghost was spreading its wings above the figure of Christ as John the Baptist raised a cup to his head, and its stillness and quiet led to how I felt at the end of Bresson's film that led in turn to when I was a child in the little church where I would light a candle at the side of the alter where I would look into the alcove at a small painting of a Jesus as I prayed.

I would go early before the start of the Eucharist when only a few pious old women dressed in black would sit in the empty pews, and the stillness and quiet was filled with the odor of frankincense from the thurible of the old deacon as I prayed for my father to be healed, Sunday after Sunday until my father died when I was ten and had no need to pray for him anymore or go to the church again.

And it was around then I had fallen in love with paintings and the years would pass until the day in the National Gallery that had become like a church when I thought of Bresson's film, and yet a painting was a picture of a moment in time, while a film was a motion picture that would attain the same effect with movement, but why attain anything? What was art and why did I need it as I once needed to pray?

Meanwhile there were in the other rooms of the Gallery my other favorites in their own quiet, the grand *Bathers at Asnieres* by Seurat that was influenced by Piero, and Rembrandt's intimate view of his young Hendrickje posing for his *Woman Bathing in a Stream*, and Degas' large and luminous *Woman Drying Herself After the Bath* that was supreme among his nudes, each with its own kind of baptism as if washed by a vision that would open my heart.

Part of Bresson's film was of a girl *Marie* who was in love with the donkey as in *"mythology,"* and after she was raped and died from shame, her father died from grief and her mother said to the rapist to leave the donkey she called a *"saint,"* and the allusions were to *The Golden Ass* of Apuleius and *The Idiot* by Dostoyevsky, though I wouldn't learn this for years.

I never saw Peter Harcourt again after the morning we watched the film and he returned to Canada, nor would I teach again after I returned to the States, yet I would continue to see it in the rest of my life when it would always have the same effect on me.

"Everyone who sees this film will be absolutely astonished," said Jean-Luc Godard, "because it is really the world in an hour and a half."

However, Ingmar Bergman said "It was completely boring" and he "didn't understand a word of it."

And the critic Pauline Kael said, "Others may find it painstakingly tedious and offensively holy".

But I would always feel the same as another critic Manohla Dargis who said it was "one of the greatest films in history," though I couldn't explain why.

Why did it make me feel as when I would light a candle for

my father? Why did I love him so deeply when he would wrap his arm around my shoulder while I curled at his side and held his other hand that was paralyzed, his eyes soft and gentle like those of a donkey and a saint?

The story in *The Golden Ass* that moved me the most was of the girl Psyche in love with Aphrodite's son and her search to find him, and I thought of her as the girl of my soul in my own search to find her or I would go mad like the prince in *The Idiot*. And it was in that fall of 1966 that I moved from my digs in the East End when Ian, the projectionist at the BFI, said there was a room open in the house he shared on Whittlesey Street in the South End near Waterloo Station with Amina a student from Egypt and Sean Hudson who was a cinematographer, and their rooms were upstairs while I would sit at my typewriter that was so near the sidewalk of the narrow lane the postman could hand me the mail through the window.

It was a cozy little house in a quiet neighborhood and my part-time teaching was pure pleasure while London was in its heyday, yet on the other side of my gratitude I was sinking deeper in my darkness as I continued to work on my book.

I had been writing it for six years from when it started with my father before his stroke, and I was trying to turn it into a novel as if my persona could be the main character, yet who was my I and what was my story really about, and unable to see it clearly I plunged blindly into my lines as I had since I was a boy when my stories first began after my father died as if I were speaking to his ghost.

I was three and a half when he was crippled by his stroke and when I couldn't understand his broken speech he didn't speak to me nor I to him and we would simply sit in silence on the little couch in the kitchen between the four-legged gas range and the radiator by the window. Then when he would drag his foot with his cane through the railroad rooms of our little apartment he would sit by the parlor window and I could see him looking down at me as I played in the street below.

I knew he loved me from how warm his arm was around my shoulder and the afternoon I came home from school when he nodded to the napkin on the kitchen table where he had scrawled my name in English with his good left hand, and then the look in his eyes when I stood at his side in the charity ward of the hospital as he lay dying. I never believed in God though I needed to when I would pray for him, and after he died the need would remain unfulfilled.

By the time I settled at Whittlesey Street my book had joined my mother with my father and the death march that sent them to where my brother and I were born. If only I could turn the horror into a vision in the same way Bresson wanted his film to be like Piero's *Baptism*, and it was then I met Bernie who lived around the corner on Roupel Street when her crocus had sprouted in her little garden, and one afternoon when we were walking home from seeing Olivier in Strindberg's *Dance of Death* in the Old Vic that was only a few blocks from where we lived, she questioned why art was so full of suffering.

Her warm brown eyes and wide smile had saved me from my woman blues, at least until I would return to the States, and she had helped to dispel my darkness with her radiance. She was a bright soul who loved helping people, and years later she would spearhead the drive to save the South Bank from the development that wanted to demolish the neighborhoods, and after she died a park would be dedicated in her name, *Bernie Spain Gardens.* She would die by suicide after several misfortunes, and her body would be found in the snow in the mountains of the Cairngorms in Scotland after she disappeared, and when her friend Ros wrote me this I would remember the dawn she returned from a trip up north and walked from Waterloo Station to my room and she climbed through the window and crouched on my phallus while I was still half asleep as if in a dream where she was like the Holy Ghost rising above me in the high of our coitus.

I had met her though Sean who was to work with Ken Loach on a film called *Kes,* and I was drawn into their circle of friends where I found the quiet I needed to work on the genocide in my book while the war in Vietnam was flaming into another holocaust.

Bresson was born at the dawn of a century of genocide and

he matured as an artist in a German prison after fighting in the French resistance and then made his first masterpiece, *Un condamne a mort s'est e'chappe, A Man Escaped* in 1956, the same year his younger contemporary Alain Resnais made *Nuit et Brouillard, Night and Fog,* which would be for me the most important film of the century when I first saw it in the new National Film Theatre near Waterloo where I walked outside and gazed at the Thames struck dumb with awe.

And yet it was a small work only a half hour long, as if it had been distilled from the history of film itself from the start of the century with the Lumiere brothers to when the Nazi footage was found before the S.S. could destroy what Resnais would save and Truffaut would call "The greatest film ever made," its delicate music and haunting narrative in counterpoint to the mounds of hair and the bodies bulldozed in a ditch. Look, it said, here is the genocide turned into art so moving you can't look away, here is the horror made into a song like an anonymous lyric you will never forget.

And it was Resnais' kyrie to remembrance that I felt Bresson would follow a decade later with the tingling sheep bells by the dying Balthazar, the grass of the field the same as on the tracks to Auschwitz that had become a museum like a gallery.

Unable to finish my book, I had sent my work in progress to a writing fellowship in California that was later granted, and I left London thinking I could return, but I would stay in California where my darkness led to a breakdown like a sickness that would cripple me, nor could I finish my book while I was falling apart and three years would pass by the end of the decade that would be called the *Sixties* while the horror in Vietnam was splitting the country apart. Then one evening the new Pacific Film Archive at the University of California in Berkeley showed Bresson's *Balthazar,* and moved by it again I came home to where I was living on Addison Street with my typewriter by another window and my book still undone.

It was supposed to be a novel like those I wanted to imitate, but I was not a novelist and even fiction writing was not natural to me. I had no talent for inventing characters with dialogue and a plot, and even my persona was no different from the I in my journal. A poet could use an I as if it were an identity and I too worked on my sentences as if they were verse, but lost in my darkness I felt blind not only to what I was writing but why I was writing.

I had devoted my life to a no money work instead of a profession that could lead to the home and family I had always longed for, and yet it was not a choice but a need as deep as when my mother first handed me a nickel to light a candle for my father. "Here," she said in Armenian, "say *aghot*, a prayer, to *Asdvas Dada, God the father*, for your father to be well again."

She never went to the church herself but had her own personal faith, yet she observed the rites of her tribe, and I followed my brother who led the way to the little Orthodox Apostolic church where he showed me the brass box to drop my nickel and then left me alone as I looked up as if there were somewhere beyond the candles that could not only make my father well but as if it really did exist, and I would continue this ritual for the next five years until he died when I didn't need to anymore, yet his death would stay inside me in a void I couldn't fill.

I had sent my manuscript to Pantheon Books in New York via the same friend, Norm Fruchter, who once led me to the BFI and now to his own friend, the editor Andre Schifrin, whose assistant, Paula McGuire, encouraged me to finish it, her note arriving as I was falling apart and had seen Bresson's *Balthazar* again in the Pacific Film Archives with the donkey's eyes like my father's that made me cry.

And it was the crying of my breakdown that would untie the knots that had crippled me and washed my eyes like a baptism as if it were the crying of the centuries of genocides and the nightmare of history. My breakdown had started from a break-up with a woman that was not its real cause but like a crack of a seizure from deep in the prehistory of my father's stroke when my mother left to care for him as if she had abandoned me.

I had no memory of the stroke but only later when one day she was washing in the kitchen sink and had turned her back to my tantrum as I pulled at her skirt, and I turned and kicked my father in the shin as he sat impotent on the little couch as if to get back at her, and the wince of tears in his eyes would sear me with guilt in the horror of my rage.

With Paula's encouragement and the weeks of crying, I slowly recovered and finished my book, yet it was not until the very last sentence when what it was truly about would dawn on me. Its plot had evolved over the years in a peregrination of dead ends and false starts, and when I tried to force an ending in surrender, Paula said no, I had to try again.

It was a family story with the genocide in the background, but I had yet to see what held it together, and I came to the last page with the same void behind the candles in my childhood prayer, and I was going to end with despair when suddenly out of nowhere I said to the ghost of my father, *I'm not going to be crippled!* And he said, *My son, I never wanted you to be; why did you think I did?* And after Paula said okay, Pantheon paid me a thousand dollars that would be much more nowadays, and I paid back the loan I had borrowed for my Reichian therapist and could start another book, and though there would come another breakdown from a break-up with another woman and more crying for years to come, I would see Balthazar again and again with his suffering transformed in an illumination like Piero's *Baptism.*

The No Money Work

One day years ago when I was out of work and feeling low, my friend Lenny Silverberg was about to teach a six week-six hour a day summer life study class at the California College of Arts and Crafts, and I asked if I could join without paying.

I had by then learned how to contour in pencil from Nicolaides' *The Natural Way to Draw*, and after Lenny's okay I went to the first session in the carriage house where a young model reclined on the platform only a few feet from where I sat on my drawing horse, and when Lenny saw me struggle with my pencil, he said:

"Why don't you try charcoal? It may be easier for you."

I didn't know how to use charcoal, I said, since I read only the beginning of Nicolaides and not about drawing in mass.

"It's very easy," Lenny said. "Here, let me show you."

Then breaking in half a stick of compressed charcoal and holding it sideways, he formed the curve of the model's breast as if he were caressing it.

She had full and luscious breasts that glowed in the natural light, and Nicolaides had said the natural way to draw was to feel what you see.

"Here," Lenny said as he stood up, "you try it."

So, returning to my drawing horse with the half of the charcoal stick, I too palmed the model's breast as if feeling it, and when it suddenly appeared on my paper it was *Eureka* with an exclamation point!

And the rest is history, as the saying goes, since it was not just a drawing horse I was sitting on, or the kundalini up my spine from the model's areola, it was the horse in me who would cure my blues, and in the following days the charcoal led to pastels, until I returned for the next six weeks like a Percival who had just discovered the holy grail.

Came the fall I enrolled in an oil painting class at Laney Community College taught by the late June Steingart who was my mother's age, and like a mother she showed me not only how to use a brush and a palette and palette knife, but opened the door to the rest of my life.

Then moving my bed to the side of the kitchen and turning my bedroom into a studio, I lived on the dole until my friend Leo Litwak found me a part-time writing workshop to teach at San Francisco State, and I painted day and night, until one weekend when I visited my mother, she watched me at my easel in her garage and said sadly in English:

"You turned from one no-money work to another no-money work, and now no woman will want you and you will never have a family."

But there was no turning back; I was now forty-three, yet as if still in puberty with so much to learn, I hurried to work as if pushed by a force that was alien to the wife and family my mother said I wouldn't have, and I kept painting whether the model was a sexy young woman or an old man with fungal toenails.

I was of course not just learning the art of painting, but what it meant. I knew what art meant in writing with the sound and sense of words, and now I would learn it in space and light while the years passed with models in life study and still-life in my cottage, until one day a decade later, my painter friend Henry Brandon mentioned painting plein air, and I asked if I could join him.

He said he would have to ask his painting partner, Terry St. John, and when Terry said sure, I joined them with my easel and oils in the trunk of my ancient Honda. They were seven years older than I, and friends since Berkeley High they had become painters when Henry studied with Richard Diebenkorn at C.C.A.C. and Terry with James Weeks at the San Francisco Art Institute; yet they didn't paint plein air until Terry curated the landscapes of Lou Siegrist with The Society of Six at the Oakland Museum.

Lou was around eighty then and Terry would drive him to the hills of Mt. Diablo State Park, and when Lou's son Lundy came, Terry and Lundy would drive to the other sites around the East Bay that were everywhere in those days and so scarce now.

"Lou would say landscape painting separates the men from the boys," quoted Terry when I first arrived on the scene, and it was true. The years of life study and still-life were my apprenticeship and now I would journey to where the vanishing point opened the horizon to the sky and the light flowered into an infinity of colors.

But it cost money, not only for paint and canvas but to pay the rent and my mechanic. Terry and Henry had adequate pensions but I would have to live as cheap as I could, and though I had found the grail in Lenny's workshop, it vanished as soon as I faced what I was up against.

"Can't you paint part-time," my mother said, "and have a family too?"

After surviving the death march and my father's stroke, she didn't struggle to raise me so I would be miserable. All right, paint if it makes you happy, she said, but I was back in my woman story of why I never married while facing what I was up against in art was even a bigger story.

Terry and Henry did have families whose kids were now grown, but they too faced what every artist was up against, even back in the caves where facing the wall was as vital as food and shelter and Michelangelo himself had to face in his own cave what art was really all about.

We painted outside only part of the week and then with

models in between, Terry with those he could afford in his studio while Henry and I shared them in different groups, and though we lived our other lives in the meantime, facing a blank canvas was always most important.

We painted under the old bridge in Crockett before the new one was built, and we painted in the old Presidio in San Francisco before it was developed, and in the old Safeway parking lot in Alameda by the estuary until it too was developed, and by the old Armory in Benicia and the old naval base in Marin and the marsh in Martinez where Joe DiMaggio was a boy until we had to leave there as well, always on the lookout for somewhere else.

But Diablo was our favorite, Terry and Henry with their easels

by their pick-ups and I by my Honda facing the hills and the valley as the cows ambled to their ranches and the coyotes loped in the distance, the turkey vultures gliding above and the wild grass a blaze of yellow in autumn and a glowing green in spring, the light always visionary in the magic hour as the years passed.

Twelve years to when my mother died and Terry moved to Thailand, and after Henry stopped painting outdoors, I painted alone by the cove at the Berkeley Marina and on Second Street by the factories.

Terry had been painting for fifty years when he moved to

Thailand with his new Thai girlfriend, and he had so many paintings by then he had to dump three truckloads. His gallery did store a bunch and he stored others with friends, but there were still three truckloads left over.

Henry's house and garage were also full when he was moving to Florida to be near his son, and he too thought of dumping them when I said, "Henry, you can afford to store them in Florida; don't think of what will happen to them; just keep painting."

When my cottage was being sold and I had to move to this bungalow, it had a garage for my own paintings, but I too had to discard stacks of my works on paper in the recycling bins, and who knows what will happen to the rest when I'm gone? Some Tibetan artists shape their mandalas in sand like children with castles on a beach that the waves will wash away, and even Shakespeare will disappear, said Virginia Woolf in *To the Lighthouse*. "The artist is one who dares to fail," wrote Beckett.

Yet "the impulse to draw is as natural as the impulse to speak," said Nicolaides, and my own had begun when I penciled a horse on the wall by my bed before I could even write, and though I stopped when I began to write, the need to draw that horse again stayed inside me, until it surfaced in my middle age when I wrote a novel about a painter imagining his grandmother whose face his mother couldn't remember.

She disappeared on a death march with her son who was modeled on my mother's older brother whom she remembered always drawing, and he must have had some talent since she recalled he drew for the church when they lived in town.

They lived on their vineyard from spring to when they returned to Adana in the rainy season where they lived in one room in a tenement, so his drawing must have been in that room and wherever he might draw in the vineyard while helping with the garden and the vines.

Yet who knows what his peasant life may have been like before my mother never saw him again? I'll never know him, yet I know his need to draw was the same as in the peasant boyhoods of Giotto and Fra Lippo Lippi and even Arshile Gorky who was his age and held his mother in his arms when she starved to death. "He loved drawing very much," was all Degas wanted on his grave, and my uncle's grave is now somewhere in the rubble between Aleppo and Damascus and the bones in the Syrian desert.

I paint it by the meadow at the Berkeley Marina. I'm as old now as old Lou who said it separates the men from the boys, yet like the mythical Percival who would never find the grail after losing it, I have to keep searching.

The meadow was where we would dump our rubble at the shore of the bay when I lived with a commune fifty years ago, and after a wilderness flourished from the landfill, a generation of nature lovers and U.C. Berkeley botany students would stroll and study the different flora and fauna, until the Santa Fe railroad sold the property to the state, thanks to a group started by Silvia McLaughlin, for whom it is now named as if it is a so-called "habitat restoration project," though it has virtually become a private nursery of a special interest group that includes some members of the local Audubon Society who have surrounded it with a fence to keep the public out.

I protested with Silvia herself before she died, and I was with her when she said to the new group:

"I didn't work so hard to lock people out."

But she died, and I now have to paint outside the fence, where her name is by the Keep Out sign, the flocks of blackbirds and the hovering kestrels all gone after the special interest group clear cut the original wilderness. Sometimes I include the fence in my compositions, since art can include anything, even a concentration camp.

Once again, I stand with my easel facing the earth and sky as if they are my mother and father in the rolling hills and looming clouds, though they are really inside me as their colors keep changing. Color is light, said Cezanne, but I can never catch its glow like Apollo failing to rape the Dawn before she hardens into a laurel tree.

I grew up with landscape painting, though I didn't know until I was grown that it rooted the art of my time when Pollack and deKooning and Kline and Gorky himself were all in essence landscape painters who descended from Cezanne's cubes and spheres where all painting stemmed between an up and a down.

Facing the vanishing point in the horizon between the hills and the meadow, I am what my uncle would have been while the clouds morph like Zeus in his lust and the hills lie behind the meadow like a nude, all my years of perspective and proportion at play with the luscious oils in memory of Terry with his big pastry spreader knife spreading his huge canvas in an orgy of colors while Henry pecked and dabbed in his gluttony for pattern and design.

A passerby stops to chat: "I used to paint," she says, "but I had to work to raise a family." She'll get back into it when she retires; she's always loved it.

There are millions of her everywhere, but what have I done with my life instead of raising a family, what is the action of my story? The daily news fills with misery and madness while my painting can't pay my new rent, and with my annual income only $12,000 a year my savings are running out. I'm turning eighty and my years are running out like the polar bears and the elephants and the planet itself. Where is the grail I lost when I found what I was up against?

My mother was right; I chose a life of no money work, yet it was with her help. I was her darling who could do whatever I wanted, but I wanted a father and became like him a kind of cripple.

I was a healthy child blessed with a great mother, until she had to leave me because of his stroke, and I wandered from her kitchen to a life of loneliness and longing.

The waxing moon rises in a royal blue above the whales of clouds and the meadow glows like the Daphne I can't catch, the fence my impasse and dead end. Speak, words, in my need to tell my story like the end of *The Horse's Mouth* where a mother nun tells Gulley not to speak because of his stroke that was like my father's when I prayed to a God that didn't exist to make him whole again, the nun telling Gulley he must pray instead of laughing and he says: "Same thing, Mother."

He was my hero when I moved to Spitalfields near his boat with my portable Underwood instead of a paintbrush. Artist meant painter, but a writer was also an artist, though twenty years would pass before I could be both like Gulley's own hero, Blake.

My need to write was the same as the need for the sky to heal my father like myself from why I would never marry and have a family, and with my Underwood on a fruit-crate and my stew cooking on a paraffin heater in my Raskolnikov attic, I worked on my first novel about my father and what crippled me.

I had wanted to be an artist since I drew a horse on the wall by my bed and then lost the boat I made in kindergarten when trying to sail it in the sewer beneath the grate by the curb, I dropped the string and it sailed into the underworld like Lawrence's *Ship of Death*.

Artist meant my longing for the sky and falling in love with Saroyan's *Daring Young Man on the Flying Trapeze* who starved to death like the suicides of *Martin Eden* and Hart Crane whose *Voyages* ended with *the seal's wide spindrift gaze toward paradise*.

So too did I want to die, yet I kept writing as if words would save me like Piero's *Baptism* in The National Gallery in Trafalgar Square washed clean from my *Slough of Despond*.

A boy approaches and wants to watch how I butter my sky and meadow with the yellows and blues of my memories. He is my uncle, watching me survey the winter weeds as if they are the history of my no money work.

He is part black and brown and white like the African-American and Hispanic and Arabic kids I sub in the Oakland public schools.

Where is he from, and he says Berkeley. He's waiting for his mother who is parked by the road and has gone to the restroom in the Doubletree Hotel. He is the grandchild I never had, and when his mother arrives she is an attractive woman wearing earrings like the daughter I never had, and they leave.

The sun is sinking behind the clouds that flame like the apocalypse at the end of Blake's *Jerusalem,* only a few minutes left of the golden rays like the end of my life.

It sinks below the horizon and the clouds darken with deep purples like a bruise so beautiful I want to sink in them and never wake, darker and darker until the darkness swallows them and I must face another night alone, always alone.

I can't paint the night; it would be like trying to paint death: my father dying in a charity ward with his eyes looking at me like pebbles in water; my mother looking at me before she died when I didn't know if she knew me or not.

Seventy years have I lived/ and never have I danced for joy, wrote Yeats.

There is no joy as long as I am an I. I longed for it since I was a boy, and now I am an old man in a winter's night, failing again to catch the glow.

Try again, says the ghost of my uncle in the nightmare of history, *the artist is one who dares to fail.*

Awake, awake, O sleeper in the land of shadows, wrote Blake, *wake! expand! I am in you and you in me, mutual in love divine.*

Yellow

"She's beautiful," I said.

"He," Bill said.

"Right," I said, "I always think of them as feminine."

I was brushing him with the curry comb, and his flank was warm and smooth and his eyes big and soft like a romantic heroine.

Even with his penis he was all grace and poise like a Degas ballerina, and I too wanted to paint him like a girl balanced on her toe, my ancient love returning to when I was a child penciling him on the wall by my bed that my mother would leave until her Saturday cleaning when she would wipe him away and let me draw again.

I was five years old and I had just seen him in a cowboy movie in the little theatre down the block with Roy Rogers, whose horse, *Trigger,* was also a palomino. Then I would see him brown with a black mane wearing a burlap and harnessed to the ice-man's cart like a god who was made a slave, the delicious odor of his nuggets steaming on the cobbles by the trolley tracks and the plumes of his breath like a blessing on my little hand.

Bill too was a city boy and had always lived in cities until he could afford a fixer-upper with his wife in Verdi, a little hamlet near Reno in the shadow of the Sierras where his corral was big enough not only for "Yellow" but also "Rocky," the wild grey and white mustang he had bought cheap and then tamed.

He pulled them in their trailer with his truck to the trail up the mountain where he would ride Rocky and give Yellow to me, and since I had never ridden before he showed me how to hold his mane and slip my sneaker into the stirrup and climb into the saddle.

"You look like you've been doing this all your life," he said.

"I have," I said, "I've been watching it in all those westerns since I was a kid."

"Just hold the reins loose and let him lead you."

He knew the trail, Bill said, and Bill and Rocky would follow us.

"Don't let him eat," Bill said when he stopped to munch a tuft of grass near the trail.

"Why?" I said.

"He's working," Bill said. "We'll feed him when we stop; just keep him at a steady pace."

But he stopped to munch again, and he was too powerful for me to pull him away.

"You're spoiling him," Bill said.

And when he started to gallop I had to pull the reins to keep him from galloping too far. Then sitting with my back straight like I would on a meditation pillow, I felt his energy rise up my spine to the top of my head.

"Pure life," Virginia Woolf called it, the same pulse and power of D.H. Lawrence's horse in *St. Mawr* and the myth of the centaur.

"How old is he?" I asked Bill.

"Twenty," he said.

"How long can he live?"

"He can live to thirty."

"He still feels strong," I said.

"He is," Bill said.

And feeling him under me like my other half that I always wanted to write about, I had fallen in love with him, the pure life of my longing while my body aged toward death. He was twenty years old like I was sixty and his own life was half gone, yet he was still strong enough to carry me up the mountain.

We rode up the trail with the big pines leading to the lodgepole like in the Peckinpah film, *Ride the High Country*. We were as old now as the actors Joel McCrea and Randolph Scott and the mountain was in the same range, and Bill quoted what McCrea said to Scott as they rode toward where McCrea would be killed:

"I just want to go to my death justified."

It was a great film, and Bill and I loved it with the other half of us that loved books and films and was part of the life in the valley below.

We were high enough now to see the valley spread into the

city as if from the mountain peak in the Buddhist metaphor of enlightenment that would rise above samsara while still rooted in *dukkha,* the air now clean and clear like laughing gas.

I visited Bill only once a year in those days, and it was always like a holiday from my life in Berkeley when I would time it to fit into his weekends away from his law practice in Reno. He too had been a writer in our youth, but he had given it up to become an attorney.

The last time I came he had just bought a small motor boat and towed it to a lake to try it out, and it was also my first time in a motorboat. He was only three years older than I but I always thought of him as a big brother who would teach me new experiences, and I had loved him from the first day we met back in Rutgers.

Kerouac had just published *On the Road* and Bill was the first of our Rutgers gang to hitch across country that would later lead to my own trip, and he had worked his way abroad on a steamer and lived in the Latin Quarter with Gregory Corso in "the Beat Hotel" on Rue Git-le-Coeur where I would also try to find a room; then living in Paris he befriended James Baldwin and William Burroughs and James Jones, and when he returned to the States he introduced me to Baldwin and gave me Jones' old trench coat with all those buttons and lapels that Jones had given to him.

I moved to London after he returned to the States, and he wrote to me when he was in Reno. He had loved the west from when he hitched there, but he was still restless and asked if I could help him move to London, and since I was leaving for Stanford I gave him my film teaching job and my digs in Spitalfields; then I didn't see him until four or was it five years later when he had passed the bar and was living with his first wife in North Beach.

He had been drinking heavily since he left Rutgers, especially when he was in Mijas in Spain where wine was so cheap, and though he had become an alcoholic he hadn't joined AA until I came to Berkeley, and I gave him three hundred dollars for a "funny farm" to dry out. It helped for a while, but it was a long haul to leave his wife and find his new one in AA, which was around the time he got lucky with a lawsuit and bought the fixer upper in Verdi and learned how to keep a horse and even tame one.

We rode until we were almost at the crest where we stopped for lunch by a stream, and I helped him strap the front ankles of Yellow and Rocky so they wouldn't move; then we fed them with the canvas bags of oats that they nibbled and munched in that delicious way animals have when they eat, their big hairy lips so endearing I wanted to kiss them the way I wanted to kiss my mother who had become like them in the nursing home where her body was shrinking as if back into the realm of rocks and trees.

The horses were like my mother and my mother and they were like the aspen and the chokecherry and the scattered pine cones where we sat on some rocks and ate the tuna fish sandwiches I had made in the morning with celery and mayonnaise, the pattern of the little twigs by my foot the same as the swirl of galaxies.

Then how delicious were the tuna fish and the slices of tomato on the rye bread and the death of the fish, and the tomato seeds and rye seeds were like the death of stars and my mother's and Bill's and mine.

"We should have bought some chocolate," Bill said, and we sucked little hard candies with water from our canteens instead. We had been riding for about three hours and Bill was impressed that I wasn't tired or sore.

I wish I could write our dialogue now like Hemingway with his friend Bill in *The Sun Also Rises,* but I can't; no one could really, not with the same music he worked so hard to perfect.

Bill loved him as much as I and said he was like a father to us, despite the sickness of his killing and what made him kill even himself. Bill too had lost his father as a kid, and like so many of our fatherless generation we adopted Hemingway's own generation who were the age of our fathers. We were in the high country with the horses and the wildlife, but we still remembered the years of books and cities.

Then we hit the trail again, and as it circled the peak, my

trust in Yellow vied with my fear of heights while his hooves clicked on the narrow trail so close to the edge. Hiking on foot I wouldn't have been afraid, but riding so high on his back, I had to keep from looking down at the great expanse that lay so far below, and I felt like a falcon perched on a crag.

My life was in his hands now, which meant on his back, and he seemed to know it. His brain was smaller than a dog's, Bill had said, or the part dogs share with us, but there was the other part Lawrence was always writing about that Hemingway couldn't, the deeper part in a horse when he carries someone like me so close to the edge, as if it would guide me home.

Then he stopped and I almost tapped him to continue before I remembered that he would stop when he wanted to shit, and as I looked back sure enough his tail was up, and the turds dropped in that happy way that would look disgusting had they come from a human.

It was hot in the open now, and my lower half hugged him close while the rest of me bobbed with the rise and fall of my breath. What pleasure could be more satisfying? With a woman maybe, but he was my woman now, so warm and full of life.

Then the trail turned and we looped down into the trees where he wanted to gallop, and it felt exciting when I let him, except for my balls that I had to keep pulling up so they wouldn't bump on the saddle because I didn't know how to ride smoothly. Was that why some women loved to ride, that bump between their legs?

Some men are afraid of horses, Bill said. They don't want to lose control to someone more powerful, but women often feel the opposite. They love that kind of power, he said, and can surrender to it.

Maybe I was like a woman, since I too surrendered to it, at least with Yellow, and it was not surrendering to the bigger Yellow that had caused me so much loneliness and despair.

We swayed and bobbed, my old friend Bill and I, riding down the trail on our exciting horses, two old men like Randolph Scott and Joel McCrea, until we returned to the truck and looked up to where we had been.

We had been riding for six hours, and I felt high with my achievement.

"You did good," Bill said, my dear friend Bill who was like a big brother.

"Thanks to you," I said.

It would be the last time I would see him.

I couldn't make it the following year; I had planned as always to drive up to see him at the end of summer, but he kept postponing my trip until autumn when I couldn't make it, so I was going to wait until the next year when he suddenly died.

He had lymphoma, I learned later, and his wife, who didn't know me well, didn't let me know he was in the hospital. Nor did she let me know of the wake, maybe because she thought oue mutual friend Beate would tell me, but Beate didn't either, and I didn't learn of it until a week later.

And so, I didn't get to say how much he meant to me until I began writing these lines about his horse Yellow. He had loved horses from way back when his friend Polk trained them in Virginia, and he later wrote a story when he was still in law school about how it felt to kiss one, and I saw the story come true when I watched him kiss Rocky.

"Hey, Big Fella!" he said one afternoon when he was approaching the corral where Rocky had lowered his head to greet him, and he kissed him on his big and hairy lips.

He loved to kiss what he loved and even slobbered me once on my cheek one night in London when he was very drunk and dragged me through Soho looking for one of his girlfriends.

He had lots of girlfriends and was never without a woman. He was blessed with good looks and a cheerful personality, but he didn't stay with any of them until he met Joan in AA and settled down with her in Verdi. He was around fifty by then and she was about ten years younger, and they did try to have a kid, but it didn't happen.

They had each other instead, and they built their little homestead by the mountains with their dogs and cats and the chickadee who perched on the feeder on the porch, and of course Yellow and Rocky.

He had always been a nature lover even as a kid when his family moved from Queens to a suburb of Newark near a marsh where he would wander like a young Wordsworth, and though his restlessness would drive him to the cities of his drinking and addiction, he finally made it to his heart's desire.

I remember him now with as many details as in a novel, but it's a poem I really need to write, a kind of pastoral elegy with a horse instead of sheep. I don't want to write the story of his life, no, I want to write what his life meant to me.

One morning when he was staying with me at the cottage in Berkeley after leaving his ex and joining AA, he said he was going to buy a pack of cigarettes in the Yemini liquor shop around the corner, and he didn't see me following him.

Then as I watched him ask for a half pint of vodka, I said: "Don't, Bill."

And he didn't.

He never forgot that, he would say to me in the following years, not about stopping him, but why I wanted to stop him.

He was my friend and yet more. *The bird a nest, the spider a web, man friendship,* wrote Blake.

He died a year before my mother when he was only 68, and my mother died the following spring when she had turned 101; then as I drove to her burial, the green of the great valley was turning a glorious yellow that was her favorite color.

Rocky, quick oil sketch on painted paperboard.

To Norm

Dear Norm,

I just finished William Sloane's novels *To Walk the Night* and *The Edge of Running Water* that I hurried to read when I learned they had had been re-issued by NYRB Classics.

He was like a father to me when he helped to lift my suspension after I returned to the Press. The old clapboard house on the corner had become like a home with him in the attic when you and I were down in the shipping room in the basement.

He was such a warm and kind man, and when I learned he had separated from his wife I would watch him leave work in his little Karmann Ghia on the long drive upstate where I imagined he lived alone. Was he as sad and lonely as I?

Kafka too was supposed to have been a warm and friendly man with dear friends who loved him, and yet his books were tales of horror and so were Sloane's whose characters and scenes were also powerfully conceived in his brilliant prose.

But why did he write only two when only in his thirties and never again? Who was the Mr. Sloane I never really got to know? You knew him better from when you were both at Bread Loaf and you must have called him *Bill* when you hung out with him in the attic.

Meeting you at the Press when I was a freshman was actually the beginning of my life as a writer, and one of my dearest memories was of the night I saw you in the front office at the big old Underwood with your index finger tapping like a woodpecker your grandfather story that would later turn into your novel, *Coat Upon A Stick*.

One day Mr. Sloane, as I called him, though he would sign *"Bill"* in his letters, came down for a book and stopped to chat about when he was a young editor in Manhattan where a young novelist brought *"a manuscript four feet high"* that he couldn't possibly edit after he read a few inches, so the writer *"took it across the street to Scribner's where Maxwell Perkins turned it into Look Homeward Angel."*

But how could that be? I know I was always distorting

memories, but I can't believe I was making it up. And yet Wikipedia said *Look Homeward Angel* was published in 1929 and Sloane graduated from Princeton in 1929. Could he have come from the family of the old Sloane publishing house where he was editing while still an under-graduate?

You said you loved *Look Homeward Angel* and read all of Thomas Wolfe in high school, yet you couldn't anymore and you would be your own Maxwell Perkins in your own book.

It seems like destiny now that when I came to Rutgers needing part-time work I was sent to the Press where you were would be like the captain of my writing life, not only in the shipping room but in what would come after I was suspended and wanted to move to the Village and you mailed me from England where you had gone on a Fulbright the address of your friends Tim and Beate on West 10th Street, and when I rang their bell a poet who was visiting knew a room I could rent a few blocks away on the corner of West 12th Street.

It was January 1960 and the Village was still standing after Jane Jacobs saved it from being razed by Robert Moses. She lived on 11th Street near the *White Horse Tavern* while she was writing *The Death and Life of Great American Cities,* and on Perry Street around the corner from my room lived Norman Mailer who had just published *Advertisements for Myself.*

Tim had marched with him carrying placards for *Caryl Chessman* under *The Women's House of Detention,* the Art Deco building on 13th Street that would later be demolished, and Beate would pass it on her way to St. Vincent's Hospital where she was a nurse and could hear the young men shout up to their girlfriends in the windows, the hospital demolished a while ago to become luxury condos.

In the meantime, Richard Yates lived in a little flat at the triangle of 11th and Bleecker Streets where he was working on his novel *Revolutionary Road,* and I would visit him while I was in his workshop at the New School on 12th Street.

Tim had a Woodrow Wilson Fellowship at Columbia but was rarely there and like you he was writing his own novel. He told me the first time you met in Rutgers you were up all night talking non-stop as if you were long lost brothers, and like you he would also become like an older brother who I would see in the evenings after my job at the bank and on weekends.

Back in Rutgers Alan Cheuse, who was eight months older than I and a grade higher, also looked up to you and Tim, and when he came to the Village we would stroll to the *Paperback Gallery* by Sheridan Square that had the new editions as good as the hardbacks, and on East 3rd and 4th Streets were the old bookshops with those out of print for only half a buck.

One night when I wasn't working the next day, Tim and Beate and I walked to the old Penn Station that I had never seen, and its monumental space was like a cathedral, yet it too would be demolished only a few years later. And after we took the train to New Brunswick Alan drove us to Fred and Ellie Tremallo's in the graduate student housing in University Heights where we sat in the kitchen while their little Mark was asleep, and I listened as Fred and Tim and Alan talked of the novels I had yet to read feeling so far behind with the need to catch up.

Fred had turned a closet into a writing room in which he would squeeze his massive shoulders over his own novel while he was working on his Ph.D under Francis Fergusson, and at the end of spring Tim told me I should hitch to Mexico where I could live cheap on a beach in Mazatlan and write my own book.

You and he had hitched there the summer before like your friend Bill Belli who had hitched the previous summer, and it would be my own rite of passage while Tim and Beate sailed abroad with their baby Steven to join Belli in Paris, and after I couldn't settle in Mazatlan I came back to Rutgers and crashed with Alan in Tim's former flat on Prosper Street where I would see Alan hulk over his typewriter like you at the Underwood in the Press.

In the following fall Richard Yates came to Rutgers to read from his new *Revolutionary Road* and Fred and I went with him and those from the reading for drinks at Alan's, and in the following spring you mailed me your *Coat Upon a Stick* that was published by Eyre and Spottiswoode with your inscription: *18 May, 1962 Pete-For you. Hope you like it,* and the inside flap of the publisher's jacket said: "*An old man is reaching the end of his life in the poor quarter of a great city.*"

Belli was called by the draft around then, and after failing the test due to albumen in his urine he drove to see me while I was living off campus. He had been in Spain in the village of Mijas near Tim and Beate in Fuengirola, and Tim told him he had to meet me and Bill too would become like my older brother.

Vietnam was only a small paragraph buried in the news while the draft had been reduced, and I guess you got out of it after you married Rachel and moved to the big apartment on Sixth Avenue by Spring Street. I had graduated from Rutgers and I was dangling from the draft when I drove out west with my friend Gregory and stopped at Fred's in Reno where he was teaching at the U. of Nevada, and Fred told me he fell in love with his student and had to flee back east with Ellie and Mark and would teach in Philips Exeter in New Hampshire.

I was called by the draft when I was back from my trip, and after failing with a 1-Y for taking narcotics, I needed a job when you suggested I work for welfare, and my caseload was in Harlem while I was living with my mother in North Bergen, and it was in that autumn President Kennedy was shot when you were playing poker with your friends from your journal *Studies On the Left,* and when I dropped by and said I heard in my office that the shooter was a socialist you worried about the effect this would have on the left.

One night your new friend Hank Heifetz dropped by who you met on the boat after he was living in Italy, and I was so overwhelmed by his genius I adopted him as my next older brother.

Alan was also living in Lower Manhattan but he was moving uptown with Mimi, and his back hurt so bad I carried all his boxes of books up and down the flights of stairs, but it was the least I could do after he had been so generous with me.

In the meantime, Tim's money ran out in Fuengirola and you gave him the classes you were teaching at Kingsway Day College in London, and when it didn't work out he brought Beate and Steven back to the States where he found an old farmhouse in East Millstone near Rutgers, and one weekend we all slept outside by the stream, you and Rachel and Hank and Natalie and Alan and Mimi and Belli with his new girlfriend, and I snapped you all with my little *Baby Brownie* camera.

I had saved enough by then that I too could live abroad after you recommended me at Kingsway, and for my going away party I invited you all to my mother's backyard where she spread a huge feast of shish-kebab and pilaf and a cucumber and tomato salad, and we later played softball in Hudson County Park; then in September you drove me to Idlewild airport in Queens that had just been renamed for Kennedy.

Not only had you set me up at Kingsway, you led me to my new digs in Spitalfields in the East End, and in the following year you and Rachel came to London and I visited you at her parents in Richmond where her father was a botanist in Kew Gardens; then one night you brought your new friend John Froines to the Kingsway gym where we played basketball, and did you bring someone who was later also one of *The Chicago Seven*?

You moved to Brooklyn after you returned to the States, and Tim and Beate left the farmhouse to take your Sixth Avenue apartment while Hank and Natalie took the one on the floor below; Belli in the meanwhile wanted to come to London and I gave him my Spitalfields flat after I moved to Waterloo, and I would also give him my class at Hammersmith when I got the fellowship at Stanford and would return to the States.

The war in Vietnam had become a holocaust and you were so politically active that summer I saw you only the night you were cutting a film with your collective called *Newsreel.* Seven years had passed since you had led me to Tim and Beate, and suddenly my passion for her burst into flames like the horror in the news, and Tim would never be like my brother again.

You had given my manuscript to Andre Schiffrin at Pantheon who gave it to his assistant Paula McGuire who would later publish it, and in the meanwhile you had written *Single File* that is now on Amazon, published *January 1, 1970...a novel of fragments...pieces of a welfare worker's journal....*

Years earlier you had asked me for my welfare notebook of my clients in Harlem and you never returned it after I went to

London. You also never returned my favorite navy blue jacket from when we worked in the Press, yet it was the least I could give you for all you gave me. You liked clothes and one of my favorite memories was of you in London on your way back to the States when you packed your suitcase with your stack of sweaters.

I saw you only a few times in the Seventies, once during my breakdown when you were visiting Hank in Berkeley and we hiked up the hill in Strawberry Canyon where you tried to console me. I had published a novel, you said, and I should feel better about myself, and I didn't see you again for thirty years until I met you in Manhattan with Hank who came down from Hamden and I almost didn't recognize you.

You gained a few pounds and some grey streaked your hair, but you were the same Norm I always loved and I wanted to hug and kiss you, yet I was still shy with you and kept my distance while Hank led us to his favorite Chinese restaurant by Washington Square.

Hank was who you wanted to see and you would have said sorry if I alone had asked to meet you. There were too many others who wanted to meet you by then, and though we were once like family, the family was gone, including Rachel, who had been killed when she was riding her bike in Prospect Park. She and I were the same age and she would confide in me in our letters around the time of her research in biochemistry, and you thanked me for sending you these letters after she died.

Tremallo's death was around the same time, though I wouldn't know of it until Alan told me when we were at a conference. He had lost touch with Fred, but by coincidence his second wife taught with Fred at Philips Exeter and she told Alan he had died of colon cancer.

I loved Fred and so did Tim, and I once drove Tim and Beate and Steven in my '51 Ford to see him and Ellie in Maine where we dropped Hank off while Natalie was visiting her mother. Back in 1960 when Fred began working with me in the Press, he gave me for my birthday a new edition of Frazer's *Golden Bough* with a long inscription in the fly leaves that he ended with his fondness for me: "*You are,*" he said, " *the only one I know whose triumph in the art of literature I would not envy. In fact, your triumph would make me more whole..."*.

And yet years later, irritated by my letters during my breakdown, he would reply in a postcard: *"Grow up."* And I would never hear from him again until I was in Boston and I called wanting to see him when Ellie answered and he told her to tell me he was too busy to come to the phone, and I didn't hear about him until I heard of his death from Alan at a conference thirty years later.

I always loved Alan, and though I rarely saw him over the years, I kept in touch by email while following his book reviews, until I was shocked when I heard on NPR that he was killed in a car accident. His book about his father, *Fall Out of Heaven*, had touched me deeply, and also his warm memoir of Tim in his book of stories, *Lost and Old Rivers*. He had looked up to you in the Sixties and told me how hurt he felt by the way you reacted when he came crying at your door after he had broken up with Mimi, and he never saw you again.

Nor had you ever seen Tim again when I was on my way back from India and took the bus to where you were working with schools in Jersey City and you took a coffee break to sit with me in a cafe near your office where I asked about your friendship with Tim and you said with your gentleness that it had *"attenuated,"* and though I gathered what you meant I had to look up the word in the dictionary.

Some friendships last and some attenuate while others end when a friend dies, like Belli for whom my love grew deeper as the years passed after he became a lawyer in San Francisco and then moved to a little hamlet called Verdi near Reno where I would drive to be with him in the high country, and on my last trip he taught me how to ride one of his horses up the mountain in one of the most exciting highs of my life, and when we stopped to feed the horses and lunch under the evergreens, he said: *You are not just a friend to me, Pete, you're my brother.*

I actually met him with you before I knew who he was when you were living with him in New Brunswick and we went with the pick-up from the Press after taking books to the Post Office.

He had returned from hitching out west and must have been on his way to Italy with his friend Jerry Gorsline who happened to be the grandson of Maxwell Perkins.

He actually didn't know my address when he came back for the draft after Tim had told him to meet me; he had gone to the student center at the Douglass girls' college where I would hang out with your old girlfriend Phyliss, and we met there as if by magic.

"Are you Pete?" he said. "Are you Bill?" I said. And I never stopped loving him and got even closer to him when I helped him dry out and he met his second wife in A.A. and bought the old house in Verdi that was remodeled by his contractor friend Tom who married Beate after Bill had introduced them.

It was Tom who answered the phone when I called to ask Beate about Bill, and I was shocked when Tom said he was surprised I wasn't at the memorial.

"What?" I said.

And when I said Beate didn't even tell me he was dying, Tom, who was a big soft-spoken good-natured man, said, *"Yeh, I guess that's what friends do, they hurt each other."*

She didn't want me at the memorial while Tim was there, which hurt me even deeper after she said Tim was crying and I could have cried with him who I never stopped loving and

hadn't seen in forty years and would never see again, nor would I ever see Beate again.

I have a history of feeling hurt by friends I would never see again. One was who I loved since we lived in the flophouse on 12th Street in the Village who was also like a big brother though like Alan he was only eight months older than I, and we stayed close until we were in our forties when he invited me to his new home with his wife in Santa Fe where he took me river rafting and I was shocked when a few years later I heard he was in Berkeley and found the number where he was staying and called asking why he never let me know.

We were in our fifties by then and I had been in Armenia from where I had written to him about my digging in the earthquake, and when he said he never got my letter there was a coldness in his voice that had always been so warm to me.

"We've been friends for more than thirty years, Will," I said. And he said, *"So what?"*

I had always known of his other friends who he would never see again, yet I never thought I would become one of them. He felt, he said, that I wanted something he couldn't give, and he hung up after I held the phone in silence unable to respond. He had finally married after years of girlfriends and had settled in Santa Fe wanting a family, yet once again it didn't work out and I would never hear from him again or learn his new address. Yes, I did need something from him, I needed his love as much I loved him, and maybe even more, but why did this make him turn away?

I loved another friend my age who I looked up to in the same way and had known since he and Ros lived around the corner with Bernie in Waterloo. He was from the upper middle class and like his father he was a champ in rugby and swimming and again like his father he too became a veterinarian in Cambridge, *"since,"* as he said, *"all sons in that class followed the same professions as their fathers."* Yet no sooner did he get his degree that his father died and he would never practice nor want to be like his father or of that class, and after turning on and dropping out he was adrift until his daughter was born and he re-built an abandoned home in Battersea on a government loan where his next daughter was born, and his third daughter was born after he sold the home and rebuilt a crumbling farmhouse in Norfolk where his ancestors were from, and in the meanwhile he eked out a living teaching Iyengar Yoga with the help of his wife who hosted their weekend retreats. I had stayed with him on my trips abroad and helped him strip wall-paper in the derelict Battersea house and later painted the outside windows of the farmhouse watching in awe as he built a meditation hall brick by brick, until there came the year I sent him my book about my mother that I inscribed with how grateful I had always been for his sharing his homes and family with me.

We were seventy by then and his daughters were grown and his wife had left after he had fallen in love with one of his students who later also left, and he was living alone after the farmhouse was sold and I didn't hear from him after I sent him my book. We had email by then and I kept emailing him until he finally replied saying yes, he got my book and then only the sentence: *"Your want is too great."*

Stunned by his sudden coldness, I replied in shock with a long blather that I also sent to Ros with whom he said he stayed close, and he replied in anger that was like a knife in my heart: *"You don't get it, do you? You're a leech."*

His yoga students were so widespread by then he held retreats from England to Spain, and when I Googled an interview with him his gentle voice and Cambridge accent sounded like a guru about the spirit of the breath. Who was he whose anger was like a knife in my heart? And yet he was right; my want really was too great and I really was like a leech.

And it was the same with the one I loved since we were in the special English class for Freshman with Paul Fussell in the Spring semester when he was one of the only seven who had the highest grades in the fall and I had to beg to be admitted after mine wasn't high enough. I was slow and looked up to his genius always feeling honored by his friendship until our senior year when we lived in a small flat on Stone Street where we had a party and invited Fussell and our revered Francis Fergusson who brought a bottle of bourbon; and after he got a Wilson to Stanford I hitched to visit him and his bright and beautiful Ellen who I idolized, and I was with them again when they came to London on his grant to write his thesis where I would crash on their couch in affluent Chiswick after it was too late for the tube to Spitalfields, and when they returned to Stanford he told me to submit my fiction for the Stegner fellowship like the one he had in poetry, and though he was gone the year I was there, I drove back east to visit the following year when he was teaching in Wellesley, and again the year I was recovering from my break-down, and then again during the winter recess when I was in Detroit, but when I wanted to come the next winter he sent a note saying sorry, he would be too busy.

I was never in the way and always in museums or libraries and even sat with their daughters when he and his wife could enjoy an evening alone, and though he was truly busy after his book *The Situation of Poetry* came out, I was taken aback by his note and didn't see him again for six years until he moved to Berkeley where he would be a full professor at the university.

He came in the summer while his family were on vacation so he could remodel the house he bought near the hills before they arrived, and I offered to help him with errands and chores so I could spend some time with him. He loved working with his hands and was expert with woodwork and I was grateful for the few moments I could share with him when we drove to the hardware and lumber shops. I loved him and treasured his humor and his genial nature, yet I was not in his class any-more, and another six years passed while I saw him only when I attended his lecture on Shakespeare and joined the dinner he gave for Alan and the drinks with Bob Hass who we knew since Stanford and Bob would take his classes at Berkeley when he went back east to teach at the University of Boston. He did send me from there a copy of his new poems in *The Want Bone* in 1990, but I would never hear him from him again and saw him only on television after he became the Poet Laureate, his good looks like a movie star.

We were sixty by then, and after we turned seventy I sent

him my book about my mother, but he didn't reply; nor did he reply after I sent him my book about my cousin Archie, his coldness a part of my old story of seeking love from someone who would turn away, my want once again like a leech.

"*My life,*" wrote Thomas Wolfe in *God's Lonely Man,* "*has been spent in solitude and wandering…Come to me, brother, in the watches of the night, come to me as you always came, bringing to me the old strength and confidence….*"

I know you won't reply, and though your friendship is gone, one of my dearest memories is of that early morning when I was a freshman and you brought me to Allan Kaprow's senior seminar where he showed slides of Picasso at the peak of his art that could be made of anything. "*Come,*" you said, as if I were your little brother, "*Kaprow won't mind.*"

Dear Cathleen

Dear Cathleen,

I wrote the following for your brother Steven after he died and I want to share with you how much you all meant to me.

Beate was three months pregnant with him in that January 1960 when I first met her and Tim in the Village with their address sent to me by Norm, who was "Norman" to us before he changed it when his first novel was published.

I knew Norm from when I was a freshman and worked as a shipping clerk in the University Press where he was my foreman and I had fallen in love with him as my new hero who I would follow like a puppy, like when we delivered books to the post office in New Brunswick and stopped at where he was living with his friend Bill Belli, and one afternoon when we were load-ing books into the pick-up, his friend Tim stopped by who was the editor of the undergrad literary journal, *Anthologist*.

Norm had been the editor in their junior year and I would save the issues Tim was editing that a lifetime later I would send to Steven in which not only Norm and Tim had their writing, but also an essay by a young professor Allan Kaprow who you can Google for how important he became with his *Happenings* that would lead to the conceptual and performance art in the years to come.

I had been in love with art since I was a kid, and one morn-ing Norm brought me to his Picasso seminar where Kaprow showed slides of how Picasso led the way to the action painting in which Kaprow himself first began as a painter. Only a few other undergrads were there that morning and one was Kaprow's protégé, Lucas Samaras, who had been Norm's roommate in their freshman dorm and Lucas' own importance can be Googled.

The art scene at Rutgers was tied to the avant garde in Manhattan only a half hour away while Norm and Tim were in an avant garde on campus, and when Norm got the Fulbright Tim won a Woodrow Wilson Fellowship to Columbia and moved to the Village to be at the center of the action.

Their one room apartment was near Sheridan Square on

West Tenth Street on the ground floor with a window facing the street and a tiny kitchen in the rear, and I had found a room for rent in a flophouse on the triangle of West Fourth and West Twelve Streets only a few blocks away.

They could afford their $110 a month with Tim's fellowship and Beate's nursing in St. Vincent's Hospital, while my room was only $7 a week that I could pay with my minimum wage job as a messenger for a bank uptown, and no sooner did I begin visiting them that I fell in love with Tim like I did with Norm who I would follow even more like a puppy.

He was only three years older yet I looked up to him as a big brother, and having no siblings he welcomed me as if I were family. He was a warm and friendly soul and Beate as well, and their cozy little home was always open to the gang from Rutgers who would come on the weekends as if it were a salon in the Left Bank or Bloomsbury in the Twenties.

Then I would have him all to myself in the evenings and the days I would take off to roam the used bookshops and galleries where I would hang on his every word as if he were my guru, and one evening he led me to a loft in midtown with a bare floor where we sat only a few feet from the actors in a new play that had just arrived in the States called *Waiting For Godot* that was known only to cognoscenti, and though I had no idea what it was about I was struck dumb by how great it was.

And it was around then he brought me to the White Horse Tavern that was in our neighborhood where Dylan Thomas drank before he died, and he said he drank there with Norman Mailer who lived on Jones Street around the corner from my flophouse and they had picketed for Caryl Chessman around The Women's House of Detention that Beate would pass on her way to St. Vincent's when she would hear the women shout from above to their boyfriends on the street below.

I had fallen in love with her as I did with Tim as if she were an older sister, but in a more distant way when I was never alone with her except by chance one night when Tim had gone to one of the jazz clubs that were then at the height of a renaissance with Coltrane and Monk and Miles and Mingus, and she lay on the bed with her belly as I sat in the canvas batwing while we listened to Bloch's Concerto Grosso on their little phonograph.

At nineteen I was very shy with women and except for a night with a prostitute I was still a virgin with no girlfriends in high-school or in Rutgers, but she put me at ease with her cheerful smile and trusted me like a younger brother while she shared her feelings about becoming a mother when she was only twenty-two.

In May when the weather was lush, Tim's fellowship finished and he would live with his parents in Camden to work in a factory and save for the trip abroad, and Beate would follow after quitting St. Vincent's. Her belly was so big by then she looked as if she were about to burst, and after Tim left she said to come for a good-bye dinner and I was embarrassed bringing only bread and cheese when she had cooked an amazing sauerbraten in the tiny kitchen that I can still taste now sixty years later.

Tim and Norm had hitched to Mexico in the previous summer that was inspired by Belli who had hitched across country the summer before, and Tim said I should do the same. "You can live on the beach in Mazatlan for almost nothing," he said.

I had saved $600 from my bank job and cheap rent, and by luck my first ride from Staten Island was with a Yale graduate in his '60 Convertible Fairlane Ford graduation gift on his way home to Memphis, and we each slept in the back seat while the other drove and we were in Memphis by the next morning; then after crossing the Mississippi I was picked up near Little Rock in Arkansas by a beautiful negro my age in a dusty old Chevy on his way to work where Governor Faubus and The Little Rock Nine would soon be in the news. Driven by my fantasy of finding a Mexican sweetheart in a grass hut on a beach in Mazatlan where I would start my novel, I was so sleepless and excited by then the rest of the trip would be like a dream with an ex-cowboy telling me his life as we careened through the green and rolling hills of the Ouchita range in east Texas and my next ride a paternal truckdriver who let me sleep beside him in his cab from Nacodoches to Houston, and at the border in Brownsville a roly-poly Mexican-American drove me on his family visit all the way to Mexico City where he dropped me off in the Zocalo, and it was there I suddenly panicked.

It could have been paradise with no smog and a blue sky and fresh pineapple every morning, but I couldn't speak Spanish and my old loneliness was so heavy I stayed only two weeks until I took the bus to Tijuana that passed Mazatlan as I looked out the window where my sweetheart and our grass hut disappeared behind me.

Tim said there was a scene in North Beach in San Francisco, but by the time I got there I lay in bed with a fever and chills in a rooming house for sailors and the summer fog was so cold and grisly I finally surrendered and hitched back east where I might get back my job at the Press and my suspension lifted, and when I stopped in Camden Tim was beaming with joy as he held his baby Steven in his arms and I saw Beate without a belly for the first time.

Tremallo was now my new foreman at the Press and Tim also looked up to him who was older than us, and one weekend Fred and I drove to Camden after Tim got the box of peyote buds he had ordered from Smith's Cactus Ranch in Texas that were so moldy and disgusting we had to eat them with pints of ice cream and Oreo cookies.

Then in September Tim had saved enough to live abroad, and when he arrived in Paris with Beate and baby Stephen, Belli told them they could live cheap on the coast of southern Spain in the little town of Fuengirola that was not yet a tourist resort where Belli would soon join them in the nearby village of Mejas, and by the end of autumn Tim was mailing me his orange and straw colored Spanish airletters about how idyllic it was.

In the meantime, I was kicked out of my room near the campus by my racist landlady after Tim's friend Bill Jones crashed on my floor when he was passing through. "You, you," she said out of breath, "let a negro sleep in my house? Get out! Get out!"

Jones and Tim had lived in a ramshackle on Prosper Street in their senior year, and Tim had left it to Alan who would let me sleep on his cot for the rest of the semester, which was when I got to know how sweet and generous Alan was, and in the following autumn Tim sent photos of the beach with his Hemingway beard and Beate's hair long like a madonna's and little Steven playing with the sand, and I would use the one of Steven in the center of a collage of baby photos for the cover of the *Anthologist* my flatmate Pinsky was editing.

In the following spring of '62 Belli was called back by his draft board but was let go because of albumen in his urine, and when he looked me up from what Tim had said about me, we bonded at first sight, and he brought me to his friend "Jimmy" Baldwin's book party for *Another Country* in Small's Paradise in Harlem, and I met Baldwin's family later in his brother's apartment.

Tim's money ran out by the end of that spring, and when Norm returned to the States he left Tim his teaching job in London, and after I graduated I too was called by the draft, but Kennedy had reduced it and they let me postpone my exam to visit who I told them was my sister's family in England, so I flew on an Icelandic turbo jet that was the cheapest flight and hitched down from Glasgow to where they were living in a nice home in Hendon in North London that would be heaped with snow in the coldest winter on record, and I would wheel little Steven in his stroller in the park who was then at the adorable age of two and a half, and I changed his diaper while Beate had to be in town and Tim was teaching in Kingsway.

Tim had Norm's Vespa by then and I hugged him tight one morning as we scootered down to Soho where he brought me to the private theatre of the British Film Institute to see the new Peckinpah film, *Guns in the Afternoon* that was *Ride the High Country* in the States about the love between the two old gunfighters.

Kingsway was headed by Fred Flower, "a great humanist educator in one of the country's most diverse further education colleges," which was connected to the British Film Institute's Education Department, and we would scooter to films all over London until one night he stayed home with Steven so Beate could see a film with me.

It was in a little theatre in Hampstead called the *Everyman* where I had to keep my knee from touching hers in the tight seats. My love for her was so obvious by now, Tim would joke about it while she took it with grace as a mother and wife, and it so happened that the film was Truffaut's new film *Jules and Jim* about two friends in love with the same woman, and the bouncy music by Delerue made us skip down to the tube station holding hands like kids that was the first time I touched her.

She was as high-spirited and adventurous as the rest of us, and when she had come to London from Spain before Kingsway began, Tim stayed with Steven for two weeks so she could hitch to Germany to visit her grandmother, and she would confide in me a buried part of her that wanted to keep going like the story of a young mother who once actually did leave her child.

At Christmas I went with Tim and his new friend from Kingsway, Gerry Wilson, who would later be my friend as well and who would write the film *Scorpio* starring Paul Scofield and Burt Lancaster, a clip of which is on YouTube with Scofield a communist like Gerry himself, and I watched as Gerry and Tim bid for a turkey at the old Smithfield Market and Beate would cook ours in the little kitchen in Hendon for our Christmas dinner where we were joined by Jim Kitses and Ann Mercer from the BFI who would later write about westerns and women in film and the warmth of our togetherness was like a scene in Dickens' *Christmas Carol.*

I stayed until the new year, and having booked my return flight from Luxembourg so I could see Paris, I went there with Tim's directions to where Belli had lived with Gregory Corso in the *Beat Hotel* at *Rue Git-le-Coeur,* and when it was full I found a room around the corner from where I could walk to the Louvre and the Jeu de Paume whose collection would later go to the Orsay.

Back in the States there was no notice from the draft, and still dangling by the end of spring '63, I was looking for a job when Norm said I could work for Welfare. He was now living on Sixth Avenue in the Soho of lower Manhattan, and one night his friend Hank Heifetz was there who worked for Welfare in South Bronx while I was in Harlem, and Hank would become my new guru whose *Origin of the Young God* by Kalidasa would later be one of the great translations of our time.

Tim needed to return to the States by the end of that spring, and by autumn he had found an old farmhouse in the pine flats of East Millstone near New Brunswick where he would work for the county welfare, but I didn't visit for a while.

Living with my mother and commuting to Harlem from her home in North Bergen, I still had no girlfriend and was down in the dumps of my old darkness when Tim called one night worrying about me. Kennedy was shot at the end of that autumn, and the winter passed with grey slush and my caseload of unwed mothers while I read the books Norm recommended, *The Other America* by Michael Harrington and Edmund Wilson's *To the Finland Station.*

In the following spring however, the snow melted as always, and by Steven's fourth birthday that was the summer solstice we all gathered at the farmhouse on the weekend: Norm and Rachel and Hank and Natalie and Alan and Mimi and Belli with his recent girlfriend, and though I was still single I was happy to be with everyone and we slept outside by the little river that was like a bucolic scene in a Renoir film.

I was free of the draft after I said I had taken narcotics, which was not a lie since Tim and I had tried heroin in the Village with the needle I borrowed from the junkie in the flophouse, and for my birthday in August I invited everyone to my mother's backyard where she made a huge feast of shish-kebab and pilaf and a cucumber and tomato salad, and Belli brought his friend Aimone whose Jamaican girlfriend hit it off with my mother as they laughed and joked like family, but alas, Beate who was fond of my mother couldn't make it because of a nursing job.

I had saved enough by then to live abroad where Tim and Norm had written to Flower for me to teach at Kingsway, and in September Norm drove me to the airport after I found a cheap flight to Rome. Hank had called his friend Giuliano Amato for me to stay the night before the train to London, and in Rome that night Giuliano gave me a short tour in his Fiat to Michelangelo's Campidoglio near the Forum that would be one of the most exciting nights of my life, and thirty years later he would be the same Giuliano who became the Prime Minister of Italy!

Norm had traded apartments in the summer with a Pop Artist in London, Gerald Laing, who made a splash with paintings of Brigit Bardot, and when Laing stayed in Manhattan, Norm pointed me to Laing's former studio in old Spitalfields near Liverpool Station from where I would send my blue airletters, and Beate who loved writing letters would always reply.

Back in America in that autumn of '64 the cultural revolution exploded with the Free Speech Movement in Berkeley and the LSD rock concerts in San Francisco, and it would spread to London already bursting its seams, so by the time I returned in the following summer to visit my mother I felt as if I had been in a whirlwind.

I had left my '51 Ford at the farmhouse while I was gone, but Beate said it went kaput, so I had to bus from North Bergen to the Port Authority Terminal in Manhattan and then to New Brunswick and hitch to East Millstone, and I made the trip only a few times that now mix in my memory with the next summer in the moil of those two years when the news of Vietnam was turning into a war.

Belli had moved to Nevada where he had a passionate affair he would describe in long letters with prose like his friend's, the novelist James Jones, and at the end of the affair he asked me to help him move to London where I left him my flat in Spitalfields after I moved to the South Bank.

Norm's wife Rachel was English and when they came to London they left their apartment in Manhattan to Tim, and when I came the next summer I helped Tim hammer away the plaster from the walls to expose the bricks in the living room that made it look warm and cozy, and after Hank and Natalie moved to the apartment on the floor below, Beate would describe in another of her great letters how Hank and Tim painted the living room with the free gallons of paint from Natalie's relative as they splashed their version of action painting that got out of hand.

Then she wrote of when you were born:

.... *I hate words when they are so dull and the joy I feel is so impossible to express. Everything about my pregnancy, delivery and post-partum was beautiful and it was the most wonderful moment in our lives. I'm so sorry I was drugged when Steven was born. Tim was the sole reason for it going so well because he believed so firmly that I could do it even when I was about to give up. But I loved him very much and it was impossible for me to do anything but go on. We watched together as Cathleen's head came through and out and then as the rest of her seemed to explode from within me. I held her blue, slimy, wriggling and screaming while the doctor cut the cord and I became ecstatic over the smell of the vernix which covered her body. I could not get enough of that fragrance and I buried my head in her neck and arms all the way to the nursery. I hated her to be washed. She was the homeliest baby there and looked, as the cleaning lady said, 'like a tough guy.' She does in fact strongly resemble Tim's father [who was a captain of a tugboat]. Tim is mostly amused by her dead-pan expressions and her funny face and really hasn't spent much time with her. I think he is content to have felt Steven's infanthood so strongly and will wait for her to grow up a bit. Steven loves her to tears. He is constantly hugging and kissing her and suffers terribly when she cries. He grows a bit impatient because she doesn't respond when he talks to her but she is his first concern when he awakens.*

But there was another side of the letter she would omit that was about what was happening between her and Tim and his drinking that I wouldn't learn until I came again in the following summer.

I had submitted the beginning of my novel for a Stegner Fellowship at Stanford in California, and after it was granted I left London and stayed the summer with my mother before driving west in a VW Bug I bought with the fellowship money, and I would take it to Manhattan where I brought Steven one day to the top of the Empire State Building, and having just turned seven he was so excited he would remember it for the rest of his life.

Tim was by now working with his friend Chuck who was a carpenter, and they would drink at night while Beate worked the evening shift at St. Vincent's, and then in the beginning of August he said he was going to drive to Mexico with his friend Dougal, which confused me since Beate would need someone to care for the kids in the evenings. They needed space from each other, he said, which seemed so sudden since I didn't know what was happening between them.

He had always enjoyed my mother's dolma and I asked her to make a pot of it for his trip that I gave to him as he and Dougal were about to drive away, and as we stood by their car on Sixth Avenue where it was easy to park in those days, he said, "Take care of my family, Pete."

"Of course," I said, and blind to what was happening I went upstairs and changed your diaper and lay you in your crib and read to Steven some Huckleberry Finn that Tim had been reading to him before his bedtime, and when Beate came home from work in her white uniform I made her an omelette and we sat at the round oak table that glowed in the colored light from the stained glass lamp by the brick wall and the windows open to the warm sultry night and the city noise from the street below, and she asked about the women I had been with in the seven years since I was a virgin in the Village.

"You know I've always been in love with you, Beate," I said, and there was a pause as we stood in the middle of the room with the slow movement of Vivaldi's guitar concerto playing on the phonograph like we once listened to Bloch's Concerto Grosso when we were alone for the first time in the Village, and suddenly our embrace was like an earthquake where the bricks fell into rubble and the next three weeks were like a delirium in a fever.

Even my mother was shocked when I came home for a change of clothes.

"You can't go back there!" she said in English, "your friend's wife is a married woman," her old guilt erupting from when she took my brother from his father when he was only four.

Pinsky and his wife Ellen were visiting their parents in Jersey and they stopped to see me in Manhattan, and when we stood by their car as they were leaving, Ellen said of Beate:

"You must take her and the kids to California."

She had just met Beate, and yet she knew her as if they were sisters.

"I could never do that to my friend," I said. "He's like a brother to me."

"He won't be your brother anymore," she said.

Beate herself told me how blind I was.

"I'll talk to Tim when he returns," I said. "He will understand."

"Oh, Pete," she said, "you don't know him at all. He will hate you."

"He will hate me?"

"What did you think?" she said.

Yet in what he would imagine that would torture him like an Othello, we were hardly alone together while Hank and Natalie were always near and friends were always dropping by, and the days passed in the fever of waiting for him to return and I went back to my mother's before driving west, and I went to see him before I left.

Beate was at work and he was standing in the living room holding you in his arms as if to tell me what happened was only an interlude and life would go on as before, and I wanted to hug him in his suffering and my betrayal of his love in my passion for his wife.

It was the so-called *Summer of Love* in Golden Gate Park in San Francisco from where I would commute to Stanford, but by the time I arrived the park was littered with garbage and the Haight-Ashbury was a tourist attraction, and I waited in a painful burning for Beate to write until her letter finally came:

....*Tim is completely broken....He began teaching in the Bronx and I think that will be a huge help in getting away from each other....I am tormented with hurting someone so much, though I know I can't not hurt him and can't live like this much longer....I either do the thing I've always done which is shut down and shut out, or else I am suddenly panicked and need more than anything else to protect him and the children and myself from inevitable end....I am so wrong, so unworthy, so guilty of the lowest of everything....I can't believe how miserable I've become....*

In January the Tet Offensive turned the war in Vietnam into a holocaust that was like a mirror of our own burning, and by the summer Manhattan had become too hard to live in, so

Tim and Hank decided to move out west where they settled in a duplex in Berkeley, and by chance I had become a mail carrier in Berkeley after my fellowship money ran out. Hank also rented a room on the other side of town to work on his novel, and I would ask him about Tim and Beate who would later move to Marin, and I wouldn't see Beate again for more than ten years except for a brief moment when she was visiting Natalie who had changed her name to Natasha.

My love for Tim was as deep as for her and still is, but losing him would leave a scar in my heart for the rest of my life. They were sweethearts when they were virgins in high school where he was a star fullback and she a talented flautist in the band, and she once told me he loved her so much it made her feel guilty, and I could only imagine how much they would suffer in staying together until you and Steven were grown.

And so those years passed until one day after the divorce when you were in high-school and Steven was on his own, I drove to see her and saw you for the first time since you were a baby, and you came in and out for only a moment like a beautiful butterfly, your eyes and your smile like your mother and yet somewhere in you like your father I could sense as well, and I wouldn't see you again until you were a mother yourself.

Beate then showed me the framed photos of her father and her childhood I had never seen before, and I wanted to hug her like a sister yet kept a distance like when we first met in the Village, and it was like meeting her again for the first time who was the same Beate and yet not the same.

A while later, Belli, who was now a lawyer in San Francisco, introduced Beate to his friend Tom, and she would marry Tom and move with him to Reno, and Belli would move nearby after his divorce and his marriage with Joan who he met in A.A., and I would drive from Berkeley and stay with Bill and Joan and see Beate and Tom in the meantime.

Steven was a father with a family of his own by now, and I had sent him a card about my Open Studio of my sculptures and he came there all the way from Marin. He enjoyed driving to the East Bay and had fond memories of living in Berkeley when he was a kid, and he remembered when I took him to the top of the Empire State Building. Hardly anyone came to my Open Studio, yet I was more than happy to sit alone with him who was the same sweet Steven I always loved as if he were my nephew.

Some time passed and not hearing from Beate in a while, I called one day when Tom answered the phone, and he said he was surprised I wasn't at Belli's funeral.

"What?" I said.

And when I said Beate never told me or that he had lymphoma, Tom, who is as you know is a good-natured person, said, "Yeh, well I guess that's what friends do, they hurt each other."

And when I reached Beate on her cell phone she was irritated by how hurt I felt as if I were blaming her. She said she was stressed by a diagnosis of a tumor in her brain, but she knew I knew the real reason was that she didn't want me at the funeral while she was there with Tim who she said was crying, which hurt me even more since it could have been the only time I might have been with him to share our grief for Bill who we loved like a brother.

He had married and built a good life in Marin near you and Steven and your kids whom he shared separately from Beate though they would see each other on special occasions, and when Steven sent him my elegy for Bill he mentioned the tumor in my ureter, which was when Alan was suddenly killed in an accident, and Tim sent me a snail mail with his old penmanship:

Pete,

I was shocked and saddened to learn of your illness, especially so close to hearing of Alan's accident. Steve's email saying that your condition may be operable is a hopeful note.

While I haven't been in touch over the years, I have thought often about those difficult times when few of us seemed to know who we were or what we were doing but also formed bonds that were more intense and exciting than many of later years. Those early days in the Village come to mind with warmth and clarity.

Over the years, I have read and admired several of your works. Steve said he is taken with one of your recent books and that he will pass it along.

Anyway, I am writing simply to say I hope you regain your health and to wish you well.

Tim

Overcome by reading this, I emailed Steven how his father was my hero, which he forwarded to Tim who sent me another snail mail that he typed this time.

Pete,

I'm sorry to hear of the pain you are experiencing and can only imagine the mental anguish you are suffering. I wish you well.

Your words to Steven were overwhelming and largely undeserved. At best I was an excited, brash young man, basking in the attention of those who listened to me. Still I wonder at how lasting the intensity and depth of those early relationships abide. I wouldn't trade the memories easily. I would trade the path I stumbled along after moving to California: one much like Belli's marked by daily drinking and confusion. I had to leave Berkeley, abandon past relationships that I found weak and lacking nourishment, and get back to my roots. There is much in Frost's poem, "Into My Own" that resonates for me.

I want you to know that I hold no rancor for all that happened in the past, though the devastation was considerable. That said, it would be impossible to try to resurrect or restore a relationship that has been in limbo nearly 50 years. The context alone would be more than difficult to define and more life consuming that either of us has time for.

"And even if we are occupied with most important things, if we attain to honor or fall into great misfortune—still let us remember how good it was once here, when we were together, united by a good and kind feeling which made us perhaps better than we are." Dostoevsky, "Karamazov."

There's no need to answer this note in kind.

Rest easy and get well

Tim

And he signed his name in pen.

He didn't hold any rancor, yet I could still feel the scar of losing him who I would never see again.

That was five years ago, and in June last year came Beate's card saying you were all hoping Steven's treatments would cure his melanoma, but after his remission she wrote in December that it had spread, and when I called her cell phone she was in the hospital and couldn't talk, and when I called the next morning she said he had died and I was sobbing as I whimpered *Oh, Beate, Oh Beate*, and when she said she and Tim sang to him the songs they sang when he was a child I kept sobbing *Oh, Beate, Oh, Beate.*

Now it is June again in these dark days of the pandemic, and I went back to what she wrote last June before Steven's diagnosis. It is one of her memoirs from her writing group that she must have shared with you, a part of it about when Steven was four months old and they were on their way to Fuengirola with Belli who was leading them there from Paris.

.... We were on the night train from Paris to Malaga, on the southern coast of Spain, the Costa del Sol; it would be another day's travel to Gibraltar and Tangier.

I dozed on and off and Steven slept on the bench rather fitfully. At one point I awakened to a lunar landscape in the moonlight, the Pyrenees had an other-worldly appearance, and I realized I was indeed entering a foreign land. The next day we arrived in Malaga in brilliant sunshine. Tim and Bill got Steven, Bill's girlfriend and me settled in a "Pensione." They rented bikes, and made the 30 kilometer ride to Fuengirola where Bill 'knew people" and would find housing for us.

Steven was sick. He had a fever and a rash spread over his body. The manager of the hostel brought a doctor or a "Practicante" (a doctor in training) to our room. He was handsome, kind, and spoke a smattering of English. He said that Steven had twenty-four-hour measles and would feel better in no time. It was true. Steven was better soon after that and the next day Tim and Bill returned, elated with the news that they had found good housing and we would take the funicular railroad to Fuengirola in the morning.

It truly seemed that we had arrived in Paradise. The rows of white-washed houses, all connected in a block, led to the glistening blue Mediterranean where small fishing boats were pulled up onto the sandy beach and the fisherman tended to their boats, sat mending nets, or lay sleeping in the shadows of their boats. Jacaranda trees dripped their fragrant lavender blooms in the town square, and donkeys, pulling their carts, brayed in the late morning streets. This would be our life which I wished could be forever.

Our house was two blocks from the sea, where we walked each day after shopping for our food at the outdoor market. We ate bocarones, calamaris, manchego cheese, and bread each day for lunch. The house had three airy bedrooms with embroidered linens, a large open living room, and a huge kitchen with white tiled floors and a generous supply of cooking pots, utensils, and dishes. There was a patio covered with vines for shade and a fig tree in the back, and tubs with built-in washboards, for washing clothes. A stairway led from the patio to an open terrace where I hung the diapers that I boiled in a large pot and where we went in the evening to look at the stars and hear the fishing boats moving out to sea. We paid $30.

A year passed quickly. Friends visited from the States [Alan Cheuse one of them] and there was a community of artists, writers, and photographers from Sweden, Denmark, Holland, England, France and Germany who got together frequently at each others' homes or at the large outdoor bar for wine and tapas with the locals. Children played and visited other tables. Women nursed their babies and Flamenco music and dancing gypsies filled the air. On Sundays, families promenaded around the town square passing the one Catholic church in town, wearing their Sunday best....

I've always loved your mother's writing like I've always loved her; it is the opposite of mine where she always writes about the bright side of life and leaves out the dark.

A couple of weeks after Steven died she emailed me:

Hi, Pete, thanks so much for your notes of concern and the lovely paintings. I'm trying to write snail mail notes to the many

*friends and family who have expressed and sent condolences. I'm
sending you a note by snail mail, because I can't bring myself to
write personal emails. It seems too cold and detached to put matters of the heart into the 'cyber-world'. Though I go through my
days doing normal things, there's always the undertone of sadness
and then the stark realization that I won't see him again. Hope
you are well. Beate.*

Then in April came her next piece for her writing group
about the little cabin Tom had built for her in Silver City, and
she had gone there during the *"Shelter in Place"* in which she
ends with the following:

*…it is peaceful, and I am content to read, write in my jour-
nal and read letters, listen to music from my collection of CD's and
cassette tapes, and finally sort through the closet full of photos, old
letters, and news clippings, put things in albums, reminisce about
my good life, and recognize my good fortune. No internet, no regular
TV, just movies and radio. Through every window I see the distant
Sierras, the Como mountains to the southeast, my garden with the
flowers beginning to bud and tiny leaves appearing on the Russian
olive and Elm tree. The wild horses roam the town like they own it
and leave their manure all over the place which we shovel into wheel
barrows for our gardens and the community garden. I am content in
my isolation and talk to Tom on the phone many times a day. And
when the weather is good, the outdoor is my home, too.…*

I wish I could write the same.

Gregory

One evening in the spring of 1963, when I was hanging out with my friend Gregory by the pool tables at the back of the bar near his home, I said:

"Gregory, let's go to California."

I was dangling from the draft and though he was exempt because of his bad knee from high school football, he too was up in the air about what to do with his life. And so, having envied me for hitching across country a few years earlier, he bought his friend Savoia's '54 Chevy for $400, and we hit the road with a big bag of his mother's choreg that we munched along the way.

We were turning twenty-three and having never been out of Jersey before, he was as excited as I once had been when we crossed the Mississippi and then after facing the blizzard in Nebraska the sun was shining by the time we hit Reno where my friend Tremallo who was teaching at the university had invited the visiting literary big shot Alfred Kazin to a party in his home.

And at the party one of Tremallo's lovely co-eds said we could crash at her home in San Francisco when she flew back for the spring break, and it turned out to be in North Beach and she was the daughter of Stanton Delapane, "a Pulitzer prize travel writer for the S.F. Chronicle who had brought Irish coffee to America," and Gregory even spent the night with her girlfriend.

Then in Berkeley, which was just a sleepy little college town in those days, we crashed for a night with my friends Smolak and Brennan from Rutgers and found from a rental board on campus a small kitchenette on the upper floor of a big rooming house on Delaware Street for only $60 a month, and we even had a party in the huge living room.

My other Rutgers friend John Ruhlman was in grad school at Cal and he showed us how to climb the fence of the swimming pool in Strawberry Canyon where we would lust at the sexy co-eds in their bathing suits, and so the weeks passed with more adventures common to the young who are footloose and free, and when I visited my friends Pinsky and Ellen in Palo Alto, Gregory hustled pool in the Cal student center and courted some co-eds while washing dishes in a fraternity house.

He had become so addicted to traveling by now he sold his Chevy to Brennan and went to Mexico with the co-eds in their summer break, and he was going to continue to South America when he suddenly heard from his sister that his grandmother was dying and he had to fly home.

He had two older sisters and a younger sister and a little brother who all grew up behind his father's and maternal grand-father's grocery shop in the West Hoboken half of Union City on the cliff looking over the river to Manhattan, and with the help of his two older sisters and Gregory working after school, his father had saved enough to buy a house with a panoramic view and his grandfather a smaller one with his grandmother and aunt.

His grandfather had come to America before the genocide and then brought his grandmother and mother, but his father was only ten during the massacre and was an orphan like my mother who didn't make it to America until after the war.

The genocide in our background was how Gregory and I became like brothers, and though we didn't meet until high-school because we were from different neighborhoods and churches, the blood tie was immediate. Ditto for our two other Armenian friends Bobby and Sahag when we were the only Armenians in our class that was mostly Italian, Irish and German.

By chance the draft had been reduced when I was called and it was easy for me to be deferred, and after I moved to London I saw Gregory only on my summer visits to my mother until I returned to the States, which was around the time Gregory him-self went abroad to Britain and Europe and even Tunisia with a Tunisian girlfriend he met in Paris when they marched with the student protesters in the riots of May '68.

He and Bobby had become social workers in Jersey City, and in '69 they flew west on their vacations and stayed in a little house I rented on Addison Street in Berkeley, and I drove them in my '60 VW Bug to Fresno where my mother was visiting my brother's in-laws.

We slept on cots in the garage and they got a big kick out of my brother's father-in-law who they called "Old Pop" and who turned out to be from the same hometown as Gregory's father!

It was a 100 degrees in Fresno and we enjoyed splashing in the little pool by the grapevines and hanging out with the neighbor's daughter, and Gregory and Bobby would later rent a car and drive the daughter and the daughter's friend to Monterey where they spent the night in a motel.

I was living in a commune the following year when Gregory came west again, but I was in bad shape and saw him for only a day and not again until the next year when I stopped in Jersey to see my mother on a trip abroad, and he and Bobby and Sahag drove me to Kennedy Airport in Sahag's new '71 Datsun, and Sahag who had two kids by now said:

"Fuckin Pete, what am I doin, I don't have a minute free, I gotta teach, I gotta go t'grad school, I gotta fix my damn house all a time, I'm a slave to my en-vye-ament; is this what life is all about?"

"Yeh," Bobby said to Sahag, "Pete doesn't know how lucky he is flying around whenever he wants, the lucky fuck."

"Yeh," Gregory said, "he really is a lucky fuck."

It was around this time that Gregory met his wife who worked with him and they would be happy together in the following years, but I was sinking lower and didn't see him or Bobby or Sahag until three years later when I drove east and stayed with Bobby since my mother had moved to Fresno by then.

One night when the four of us were at Bobby's apartment while Gregory and Sahag were playing backgammon, Bobby said to them in regard to my sexual famine:

"I got to get this fuck laid."

"Yeh," Gregory said, "get the poor guy laid, Bobby."

"Take him to the Ichi-Ban," Sahag said, "and ask Santomena if he knows any hoo-ers."

The Ichi-Ban that Santomena named from his army days in Japan was the bar and pool-room where Gregory had played pool, and Santomena had once actually given Gregory and me the address of a prostitute in Newark where we had our first sex when we were eighteen.

"Hey," Bobby said, "you just reminded me. I'll take him to Little Carl."

"Who's Little Carl?" I said.

"You remember Little Carl," Sahag said. "He was a year behind us and played tackle."

"He played guard," said Gregory, who was captain in our senior year before he hurt his knee.

"Don't tell me what he played," Sahag said, "who should know better than me, I was the fullback and had to run behind him."

"Okay," Gregory said, "but how is he going to get Pete laid?"

Little Carl, who was by now three hundred pounds, managed the new high-rise on the cliff where one of the renters was a hooker and there had once been a great view of Manhattan from this part of the cliff when we were kids, but as Bobby and I approached it was blocked by the high-rise, and Bobby said:

"Did you jerk off first?"

"No, why?"

"In case you come too soon, stupid, don't you know anything?"

"Hey, Pete," Carl said when we met him in the lobby, "Bobby tells me you need to get laid."

"He didn't jerk off first," Bobby said.

"That's all right," Carl said, "she'll give him a good time."

"How much will it be, Carl?" I said.

"Don't worry about the fucking money," Bobby said.

"No, Bobby," I said. "I can pay for my own whores."

"She's doing me a favor," Carl said. "She usually charges a hundred but she'll let you in for twenty-five."

A hundred then was like hundreds now, but she was worth it, and I didn't see Gregory and Bobby and Sahag again until three years later on my way to India, and then another two years passed before I flew east from my job in Detroit for the twentieth anniversary of our high school graduation in '78.

Then in the spring of '81 Gregory's daughter was born, and I mailed him a copy of *Grimm's Fairy Tales* that he later said he would often read to her.

He had his masters in social work by then and he was working for the V.A. in Newark as a therapist for the Vets from

Vietnam, and his wife also had a masters and they scraped enough for a home in Upper Montclair that he would later call "very happy."

In the meantime, I saw him and Bobby and Sahag only on my trips back east when I would stay in Bobby's new condominium in Manhattan on the upper West Side, and the four of us would spend a day together, once in '84 and again in '87 and '93.

But my memory blurs and I can't remember when Gregory fell from his ladder in his yard and hit his head on the concrete, and his headaches were so severe he had to take pain-killers, and a while later he had to take more pain-killers from his open-heart surgery that didn't heal right.

I had come east again and was staying in Montclair with Carmela our friend from high school since Bobby had moved, but when Gregory dropped by to see me at Carmela's he could stay only a short while due to his pain and I winced when I saw what had happened to his body.

He was a natural athlete with broad shoulders and great hands that I had envied since we were kids when he was first rate in basketball and football and baseball and tennis and ping-pong, and I would love to watch his hands even when he would roll the dice and slam the checkers in backgammon, his strong and nimble fingers still vivid in my mind's eyes from when he would spread them wide on the green of the pool table and curl them around the cue stick.

One summer when we were fifteen, he had invited me for a week in his family's summer home in the Catskills, and when I watched him swim up the creek and back I saw that he was a great swimmer too.

But now sitting in Carmela's with his broad shoulders hunched over the clench of his hands on her table, he apologized saying he wasn't feeling well and had to leave.

His marriage too had fallen apart during his medical woes and he moved to a little apartment, though he and his wife stayed close and he would drop by the house to carve his little sculptures in his basement workshop and putter in the garden and play with their cats. They had stopped sleeping together and had become like brother and sister and would have weekly dinners with their daughter.

His move to the apartment was actually when he and I grew even closer, and I stayed there three times in the following years. We were in our sixties by then and we cooked meals together like we once did on Delaware Street and adventured again to the Met in Manhattan and to the Catskills where his younger sister Sonia was living in their family home after their parents died.

His knees had become so painful he could hardly walk and the last time we went to the Met I had to wheel him in a wheel chair and take the elevator to the galleries. He loved art and he loved my own work and he hung it in his living room and kitchen.

He also loved to read since we were kids and he once read my copies of *For Whom the Bell Tolls* and *Lust for Life* while he sat in his father's grocery shop in between serving the customers, and now in his old age he loved reading books on mountain climbing, especially by Jon Krakauer.

We talked on the phone every week and sometimes twice a week for at least an hour and sometimes two hours, which was how I learned about the years of his marriage when I had seen him so rarely and he told me about falling in love with his wife and how happy they were when their daughter was born and how much his daughter meant to him.

He enjoyed hearing about the cottage where I had moved after leaving Addison Street and he got a big kick out of the bamboo growing through my floor and his laughter over the phone was a saving grace in my loneliness.

But turning seventy his troubles increased and our talk turned to his prostate surgery and the money he had to spend on his teeth and his different doctors and pain-killers, until I couldn't make him laugh anymore and when I came east again he wouldn't let me visit him.

"Gregory," I said, "I came all this way to see you."

"I'm sorry," he said.

Bobby had moved to Westchester and I was staying with Ruhlman's son Nathaniel in Manhattan from where I called

Gregory and pleaded for him to let me take the bus to Montclair and visit at least for an hour or so, but he said no, he wasn't feeling well. He would try to drive to Nathaniel's, he said, but he could barely drive by then.

He was feeling better with his new pain-killers when I returned to Berkeley, but when I tried to return to our old phone talks he apologized again saying all he could think about was what had happened to his body and talking about it made him even more depressed.

His wife's own health had declined and she couldn't afford the increasing taxes and repairs on the house while he was renting his apartment, and they had to sell it.

His daughter had turned thirty, and making a life for herself she moved to an apartment like his in the same complex, and after the house was sold his wife also found one there.

He couldn't drive anymore and they shopped for him and drove him to his different doctors and his dentist when his teeth were so bad he needed a bridge.

Then he stopped answering the phone and replying to my emails, and months went by until I emailed his sister Sonia who replied saying he was "not the same Gregory" and I should just keep my "best memories of him."

She didn't know me except for when I once visited her with Gregory, and she was irritated by my continuing to ask for a diagnosis. Their family that I had always envied had been devastated by their little brother Georgie's schizophrenia and their parents dying of grief and the cancer death of their older sister Gloria that shook Gregory especially hard.

Nor would his daughter Kristin tell me the truth in her email replies. She didn't know me except for a brief hello when I had stayed with him in his apartment, and unlike Sonia she denied there was anything wrong with him and said only that he was doing well.

His wife Kay had no email and not knowing me either, she simply didn't reply to my snail mail that I sent in care of Gregory since I didn't know her apartment number. She and Kristin had always been distant with me, and respecting their privacy

Gregory had never tried to bring us closer.

I dedicated my new book to him, but after I mailed him a copy, he sent me a little note with a check.

"6/21/17 Dear Pete," said his neat penmanship in capital letters on the blue lines of the note card, "Thanks for sending a copy of your book. It looks interesting. Bravo for your hard work. Enclosed is payment for the copy I received. Gregory"

I ripped the check and replied in reminding him of the dedication, but it was the last I would hear from him.

Panicked by Sonia's "not the same Gregory," I was afraid he might have a kind of dementia, and though I was relieved by the card that he was still lucid, I was still desperate to know what had really happened to him, and I asked Carmela to email Kristin if she could visit and then tell me what she could observe, but all Kristin replied to Carmela was that he didn't want any visitors at the moment.

I also asked Bobby to visit, but Gregory was upset when he walked in and he told Bobby to leave.

"What was he like?" I asked Bobby over the phone, but all Bobby said was that Gregory could be very moody. He was not as close to Gregory as I and Bobby was pre-occupied with his own prostate cancer.

I wanted to fly back and see him for myself, but when I wrote to his wife and Kristin if they would help me see him, they didn't reply, and in the meantime my cottage was sold and I was overwhelmed by my need to move.

I pleaded with Sonia to tell me more than that he's not the same Gregory, but all she replied was that whenever she saw him he just hung his head and barely responded and all the years of pain-killers had taken their toll on him.

But what was that toll?

I emailed Kristin again to please tell me if he could still remember me, and she replied:

"Dad is well, He's not out of it mentally, so yes, he can read a card, the newspaper, watch TV, interact etc. He's just a quiet guy these days, very sleepy. He enjoys the comforts of home and relaxing. He's medically stable and I'm sure will be for a while.

He's just a weaker guy. Thanks for checking in. Kristin"

He might be medically stable, but "very sleepy" was probably what Sonia meant by "not the same Gregory." And if he
wasn't the same, then who was he?

I sent him a self-addressed stamped envelope asking him to
send me at least a few words, and when he didn't I realized I was
asking for his love that he couldn't give me anymore, and I was
back to my same old story of my father who couldn't speak to
me when I was a child lighting a candle to the void behind the
sky.

Please, I would pray, please make my father better, and now
Gregory had become like my father and I couldn't pray anymore.

Old age, sickness and death await us all, said the Buddha,
but the path to awakening was filled with despair, and I lost
faith and courage.

Gregory, dearest Gregory, I wrote in my journal, my love for
you brings tears to my eyes and they become a flood of memories
and the great stories you would tell me over the phone, like the
one of when your brother Georgie stopped taking his pills for
his schizophrenia and he somehow made it to Las Vegas, New
Mexico instead of Nevada in search of Marilyn Monroe, and
you flew to Albuquerque and rented a car and by some miracle
found him wandering in the streets, and when he wouldn't take
the pills you brought you convinced him by taking one yourself
and it made you so dizzy that Georgie himself had to help you
on the plane to get you back to Newark where you eventually
got him into a halfway house. He was your little brother ten
years younger and you worried about him and took care of him
and he was in fact why you became a therapist as if you could
understand not only what was happening in his mind but your
own in this our unenlightened life where dream and reality are
two sides of the same coin.

Gregory, Gregory, O my Gregory, please speak to me again.

But you had become the void that never answered and I
didn't know of your death until your sister emailed me a week
later.

The I

"Don't look in the mirror too long," said my mother one day when I was a child, "it will make you *khev*," the Armenian word for *crazy*, whose guttural *kh* made it sound ominous. I was learning English then, and with her own English improving she would mix it with her Armenian. She had been a peasant as a child and still had a peasant's faith in superstitions, though there was truth in this one, and like Narcissus I too would fall victim to the mirror's image.

In the meantime, I had fallen in love with words, and by chance or what we call destiny, which in Armenian is called *jagad-akir*, *jagad* for forehead and *kir* for writing, hence: writing on the forehead, and my new language had become the English in which I would talk to myself.

I wonder now who I might have been had I begun talking to myself in Armenian. My mother's first tongue was Turkish and she didn't learn Armenian until she was freed from her internment, and I wonder if she talked to herself in a mix of Turkish and Armenian and later in her limited English?

I can't remember when I became aware of talking to myself, but it was around the time she warned me about the mirror, and I remember one day I suddenly felt alien to myself as if there was a difference between my thinking and my being. It was only a nanosecond like a flash of light as if to tell me that I didn't know who I really am, and though I would ignore it with the more urgent needs of being human, it would continue to happen in the rest of my life.

I suppose it might be tied to my father's stroke when my mother turned from me to care for him. It was in January of 1944 when I was three and a half, and soon afterwards she let me step out to the street where I began to learn American English with a West Hoboken accent.

In those days the streets were safe for small children to be left alone when there were always neighbors and shopkeepers who would keep an eye on them, and it was actually exciting since just outside the vestibule of our apartment building were the Chinese laundry shop and the Jewish delicatessen and the Italian shoemaker and the Italian tavern with a pizza parlor in the rear and all the other shops packed on that single block.

And when I was brave enough to cross the trolley tracks to the other side, there were the Italian delicatessen and the Jewish candy-store and another Italian barber and the Irish tavern, and one day that must have been in May or August of 1945, the air was filled with confetti and everyone was shouting and blowing horns for the end of the war.

I was only dimly aware of the war and yet I remember when I must have been only three in the photographer's studio he handed me a wooden rifle to pose in my toddler's army uniform and I wanted to keep the rifle.

It was the fashion then for little boys to be photographed in army or navy uniforms, and one day when reminiscing with my mother a lifetime later, I asked about the photo and she said she wasn't at the photographer's, it was my father who took me there. I had no memory of my father before he was paralyzed, yet I would remember the wooden rifle as clearly as Orson Welles' *Rosebud* in *Citizen Kane,* and as I try here now to write my own kind of movie, my personal history entwines with the First World War and the genocide that sent my mother and father to America where English became the language in which I would talk to myself.

Armenian was my first tongue from when I would mime my mother's lips speaking to me as a baby, but I never spoke it again after learning English, so I was not really bi-lingual and my Armenian today is only of a four-year old, and since I never learned its strange alphabet and I couldn't improve my vocabulary by reading it.

I wasn't good with English either, and my kindergarten best friend Denny Negrini's mother mentioned to him how poor it was. I was also a slow reader and I learned how slow as early as third grade when sitting in my desk with a story book in a silent reading lesson I noticed my friend Gary Nelson was turning his pages three times faster than I. Nevertheless, I had a special need to write my own story, why I didn't really know.

The stories in school were nowhere as good as in my comic books, but turning nine in the summer when my mother brought my father and me to a relative's farm to escape the heat in the city I didn't bring any comics, and one night when the radio wasn't working I felt like writing a story as if to entertain myself. I couldn't write any better than I could read and yet I pretended I could imitate not only my comics but the movies in the little theater back in the city with the westerns and the war films of the Forties.

Like all humans I loved stories and by seventh grade I knew that more than anything else I wanted to keep imitating them until I could write my own. Then one day after trying a couple in high school I suddenly panicked at the thought of how I would earn money after I left my mother's home, since I knew by then I would have to leave her if I were to be a man, and I decided I would go to college, not only because I was hungry for knowledge but that it might help me find work for how I would live while I continued to write.

It turned out to be easy in America in those days, at least for young men like me who cared only about writing and had no want for anything more than a simple way of life. The hard part however was my sickness, though I wouldn't be aware of it as a sickness until my first breakdown a lifetime later. It had actually started around the time my mother warned me about the mirror and the feeling alien to myself began to grow into feeling alien in a world where I felt like an outsider as if I were not good enough to belong in it.

I would survive as we all do since the life force was stronger inside me, but feeling alien would remain like a worm in the heart of my being that would surface in my teens with the opposite sex that would turn into the story of why I would never marry and have the home and family I would always envy.

A writer writes away his sickness, said D.H. Lawrence somewhere, and I was my own sickness that I would try to escape in the sea of words as if I could transform them into music and pictures with characters and a plot, and my *I* became my persona for a son with a father who was a cripple.

It began one night in the spring of 1961 after I had returned to Rutgers and moved in with Dennis Lindberg who lived on Neilson Street in New Brunswick. I had by then written the stack of sketches I had submitted to Richard Yates in the New School in the previous spring, but I had yet to write an actual story that was more than a sketch, and on that evening when Dennis was practicing his bassoon, I suddenly started writing about my father, why I didn't really know. I had read somewhere that Hemingway and Faulkner, who were two of my father figures, had once gone fishing together, and I suddenly imagined the ghost of my father sitting with them around their campfire.

I had never written about my father before, and though he was with my mother the major part of my psyche, he did not surface until one night in my freshman year when working for the University Press during the winter break I had to sleep alone in the empty dorm whose darkness frightened me, and as I lay in bed imagining a maniac killer lurking in the hallway, I suddenly remembered coming home from school when my father was as always sitting on the little couch in the kitchen we called a *sadir* that was a heavy quilt of raw wool on a storage box between the four-legged gas range and the radiator where I had once cuddled inside his good left arm, and he nodded to the napkin on the kitchen table where he had scrawled with a stub of a pencil my name in English as if to tell me he loved me, and remembering this made me suddenly burst into the same sobbing as when I was a boy after his funeral.

Not long after his funeral I had been lying in bed when I could hear my mother in the kitchen tell our neighbor Baidzar what the priest had told her at the wake about when he would see me lighting a candle by the altar when he would sit in his throne waiting to start the Liturgy and he would notice how fervently I prayed as if I were longing for something, and hearing my mother tell this to old Baidzar I had to muffle my sobbing with my pillow as if I were the boy in the priest's story feeling sorry for myself, and it was this same story I would be writing for the rest of my life whose first chapter I would begin in Dennis Lindberg's apartment while he was practicing his bassoon.

I wrote it in one sitting and then mailed it to Yates who passed it to his friend Hayes Jacob who included it in his anthology, *New Voices,* which was published by Macmillan, and so, for better or for worse I was now in the fatal game of publish or perish, and the worst wouldn't come until sixty years later when all my writing wouldn't pay for even a month's rent while my savings ran out, and I was back to the mirror my mother said would make me *khev* if I stared in it too long.

Every story needed a character and mine was my *I* that had become my persona, but who was the other *I* behind my mask in the nanosecond flash of not knowing know who I really was? My persona that had become my character had become a sickness like Milton's Satan in *Paradise Lost* who we call the *ego,* though the guttural of Freud's *Ich* sounded more ominous.

Yet in correcting Milton, Blake called it the *Selfhood* in his own *Prophecies* where God is not above but inside us in the *Human Form Divine* whose creative energy is our savior. The word for energy in Armenian, which is one of the most primal of Indo-European languages, is *uz,* pronounced *ooshz,* as in juice, and in my own story it was my *uz* that had penciled my horse on the wall by my bed around the time I fell in love with words, as if somewhere inside my fingers were following my ancestors into the caves where they had drawn their own horses on their own walls with their own carbon.

The impulse to draw, said my mentor Nicolaides, *is as natural as the impulse to speak,* and also to sing and dance and do anything creative, but it needed an *I* to begin and yet my *I* had no form or substance and was like my fear of abandonment like when I was three and lost my mother on the boardwalk and panicked until she found me.

But it wasn't she who found me, she would tell me a lifetime later, it was my father who I wouldn't be able to remember before his stroke. He was finally in 1943 making good money in the war economy and my mother could stay home from the factory for the first time since she had come to America, since even after my brother was born his grandmother would bring him to her machine while she would open her blouse to nurse him, and now that my father was selling his jewelry she could stay home and cook and clean for us and even afford a carpet for the parlor and a parlor set and even a little *Frigidaire.*

He was finally providing again like he had for his sister's family. He was a talented jeweler who could sit for hours twisting silver into intricate designs and his big gentle hands were soft and warm and even ambidextrous. He wasn't a loser, he wasn't the failure I would feel like in my own life, my father was a real man in that year before his stroke in January 1943 that I could not remember but only of sitting at his side while he let me touch the fingers of his right hand that could not move, and when he saw that I couldn't understand the slur of his words he never tried to speak to me again, nor did I ever speak to him, though when I prayed for him every Sunday it was as if he were listening.

We all have somewhere in our dark past the moment when we fell like Satan from paradise or went to sleep in the bewilderment of samsara or whatever belief we use in the story we tell ourselves about who we think we are, and I imagine mine was when my mother left me with Baidzar during those days when my brother took her back and forth to Bellevue until she brought him home and emptied his bed-pan until he could rise with his cane and drag his foot to the toilet by himself.

But one day when I was playing with his cane as if to imitate him, she suddenly shouted *"Stop that!"* as if my play were an omen that I would grow up to be a cripple. I didn't of course, yet I did need a father to imitate, and after he died when I was ten, the die of my character engraved the writing on my forehead, and I too would sit all day twisting words as if to turn them into jewelry.

But there is no *I* in jewelry or any stone or metal in the sands of time, and the *I* of whoever made a necklace or a broach or even an anonymous song or dance was like a ghost of no substance or form, though without it nothing could be made. All art needed an *I* to be created, but once it began the *uz* took over, like when we fall asleep in the realm of dreams where the *I* splits into different characters and stories depending on our histories or what drove our ancestors into the belly of a cave.

Poets use the *I* as if it is real, yet the poems that move me most are when the *I* gives way to the *uz* like when Milton invoked his muse:

...thou O spirit with mighty wing outspread, dovelike sat'st brooding on the vast Abyss and mad'st it pregnant....

The spirit is the dove of the Holy Ghost and the *chi* and the *shakti* and the *uz* in all inspired poesy, it is the *I* splitting like an atom into an expanding universe like a dream of infinite characters and scenes until they are all swallowed in the black hole of our final breath we call death that is in Armenian the more resonant *mah*.

And I am back to my mother telling me not to look in the mirror too long or it would make me *khev*, and there comes again the feeling alien to myself not knowing who I really am, and I read what Nisargadatta once said in his little attic in Bombay that was recorded and translated from Marathi into English by Maurice Friedman, a Polish Jew whose English was his fourth language.

"You are all-pervading, eternal and infinitely creative awareness. All else is local and temporary. Don't forget what you are....A person is but the sum total of memories....I ask you only to stop imagining that you were born, have a mother, will die, and so on. Just try, make a beginning—it's not as hard as you think.... As long as you are enmeshed in a particular personality you can see nothing beyond it. But as a tiny point of a pencil can draw innumerable pictures so does the dimensionless point of awareness draw the contents of the vast universe. Find that point and be free. Find what you have never lost, find the inalienable."

But I don't and I am still enmeshed in my personality that has caused me such heartache always pushing myself to keep writing and drawing as I did when I was subbing in Oakland Technical High School where I drew more sketches of the students while they chatted or watched their smart phones, and then in my free period I took my drawings to the secretary Lynette in the office to make me copies so I could give the originals and there happened to be a student passing by who said:

"You did one of me, too!"

She was yet another beautiful girl, actually a young woman already.

"I'm so sorry," I said. "I can't remember you."

"That's okay," she said. "It was three years ago when I was in ninth grade."

"Do you still have it?" I said.

"Oh, yes!" she said. "I had it framed and it's on my bedroom wall!"

And like a Painted Lady butterfly, she left as quickly as she appeared like a nanosecond flash of light as if to remind me of who I really might be.

I live for such moments.

Freud's Story

Freud's greatest story for me was his little book *Civilization and its Discontents* that he began by describing the mind like the city of Rome:

"Historians tell us that the oldest Rome was the Roma quadrata, a fenced settlement on the Palatine that was followed by the phase of the Septimontium when the colonies of the different hills united together and then the town bounded by the Servian wall, and later, after the transformations of the republic and the early Caesars, came the city that the Emperor Aurealian enclosed by his walls.

"These places are now in ruins, yet they are not of the early buildings but in restorations of them, and all that remains of ancient Rome is woven into the fabric of a great metropolis that has arisen in the last few centuries since the Renaissance.

"Now let us suppose that Rome was a mental entity in which all the earlier stages of development had survived alongside the latest, the Palatine of the Caesars and the Septizonium of Septimus Severus still towering to its old height, the beautiful statues still in the colonnade of St. Angelo as they were up to its siege by the Goths, and where the Palazzo Caffarelli would also be the Temple of Jupiter Capitolinus not merely in its latest form but in its earliest shape when it still wore its Etruscan design adorned with terra-cotta antefixae. Where the Coliseum stands now we could at the same time admire Nero's Golden House on the Piazza of the Pantheon and find not only the Pantheon of today as bequeathed to us by Hadrian, but at the same time Agrippa's original edifice instead, and the same ground would support the church of the Santa Maria sopra Minerva and the old temple over which it was built..."

All of Freud's stories were about the mind and how it was tied to the body, as in taboos of excrement and menstruation and most of all sex that he would study as a scientist, and though his *Das Unbehagen in der Kultur* was one of the darkest stories ever told, he would put in it all he knew from its first chapter about the origins of religion to its dramatic end:

"The fateful question of the human species seems to me to be whether and to what extent the cultural process developed in it will succeed in mastering the derangements of communal life caused by the human instinct of aggression and self-destruction. In this connection, perhaps the phase through which we are at this moment passing deserves special interest. Humans have brought their powers of subduing the forces of nature to such a pitch that by using them they could now very easily exterminate one another to the last person. They know this—hence arises a great part of their current unrest, their dejection, their mood of apprehension. And now it may be expected that the other of the two 'heavenly forces', eternal Eros, will put forth his strength so as to maintain himself alongside his equally immortal adversary."

He was writing in 1929 before the atom bomb and the mass extinctions of life on the planet, and yet it was the same old story told even before writing was invented. Once upon a time, it said, there was life against death in a world of light and darkness, but why was it always filled with suffering?

Once upon another time in the year after the bomb, a woman around forty walked home from the factory at day's end and climbed the three flights of stairs to the railroad rooms of the little apartment where her crippled husband sat on the small sofa between the stove and the kitchen window, her five-year old son playing with his toys on the linoleum and her sixteen-year old on his way home from his afternoon job as a soda jerk.

Her youngest in kindergarten by now, she had returned to the factory after sewing at home since her husband's stroke, and she began cooking a simple meal of bulgur pilaf with lamb bones and green beans in a garlic and tomato sauce she served with a loaf of bread from the Italian bakery, her husband lifting himself with his cane to sit at the small table with the boy and his brother who would finish eating by the time she herself sat down, the boy leaving to listen to the radio in the parlor and the teen to his club around the corner.

She had worried about the club until a friend whose son

was also there said they were just being boys. It was in a store-front with a pool table the older youth had rented on the street once called *The Dardanelles* because of the gambling cafes of the Armenian immigrants whose sons now mixed with the Italians and the Irish and Germans and some Syrians and Jews.

She herself had become international and polyglot after she lost her family on the death march when the English soldiers liberated her orphanage and brought Armenians who taught her Armenian since she had spoken only Turkish as a peas-ant child, and when she was a servant girl with an Armenian family in Beirut she learned some Arabic she would later use in America when she sewed with Syrian workers in a Syrian's factory; then after sewing with Italians she learned her broken English with their accent and was with them when they joined the *International Ladies Garment Workers Union* that cut her hours to only eight a day, which was around the time her divorce was settled when she was finally able to marry the man she loved who had come to live with her and her first born.

He was a jeweler who had a hard time selling his work during the Depression, but with the start of the second world war he began to earn enough for her to stay home with their baby, which was the first time she didn't have to work anymore, for even when her first son was born her mother-in-law would bring him to the factory for her to nurse him. Now however she could stay home with her infant in her new happiness while cities were being bombed overseas.

They were then on the first floor where she had moved as a single mother when the Italian landlord welcomed her and her child. She knew him from his other Armenian tenants and he told her he'd rather rent to Armenians than his *paisans* who might gossip about his family. His two married daughters lived on the upper floors and she would share the apartment near his with his two youngest in what would have been the parlor where they would leave the sliding door open during the heat waves so the breeze could blow through.

She had to stay single for two years when her first husband could have claimed their son since divorced women had no rights, but he didn't come to court to contest the divorce and the boy would see him and his grandmother after school since they lived only two blocks away.

Then one day one of the top floor apartments was vacant, but she balked when the landlord offered it to her.

It was bad luck, she said, to move in the same building.

"You a movin up," said the old Italian, *"not a down."*

The top floor was in fact much nicer, and from the kitchen window that was as high as the wash poles in the backyards there was a glimpse of the Empire State Building across the river and she could grow parsley in a box on the fire-escape, and from the parlor facing west at sundown the sky would be red above the rooftops. She had as a child grown up in a vineyard that was like a little Eden before the genocide, and though her life had been wrought with hardship, it now looked bright in her new happiness.

Her husband's jewelry was selling so well during the war that he could afford a new parlor set with a matching couch and sofa chair and then an oriental carpet, and one day the Armenian merchant in his appliance shop across the street wanted to sell her a *Frigidaire*. It cost too much, she said, and like a typical Armenian businessman he said she didn't have to pay it all but only a little each week.

It was the smallest model and the little freezer was barely big enough for the ice cube tray, but she wouldn't have to buy a chunk of ice from the ice-man each week and she could stuff it with her leftovers without any worry. In the meantime, she sewed new gingham curtains for the kitchen windows and a delicate lace tied with a bow in the parlor, and the war years passed while she strolled her toddler to the little park nearby and her husband would show him off to his pals.

One morning after a New Year's Eve party she told him how happy he looked as he was leaving for work. He was thirteen years older than her and she had been in love with him since she was a picture bride to her first husband who was his cousin. He had come to America as a teen when he fled the Turkish draft that would turn him into cannon fodder and his older brothers were later executed during the massacre; yet like her he had survived and endured and she now enjoyed cooking for him while he enjoyed her cooking that was rich with the fat of the lamb in their new prosperity while he looked forward to when he could move from silver to gold in his jewelry.

Yes, he said, he did feel happy as he stood by the door while she dressed their child on the little couch between the stove and the kitchen window on that last morning of her seven years of happiness.

She had seven years of happiness, she would say to a friend who had also been a picture bride to a husband she had not chosen, and the friend said she was lucky to have had seven years with a man she loved when so many others never had any.

And it was in that afternoon after he looked so happy that the message came from an Armenian neighbor who had been on the bus through the tunnel to Manhattan where he fell to the floor and the neighbor had gone with him in the ambulance to Bellevue Hospital.

She was so shocked after he was brought home that his niece who was her closest friend had to help wash him and empty his bed pan until she could recover. She had been shocked when she was torn from her mother on the death march, yet once again she would survive and endure.

The stroke said the doctor was so massive he would either die or live for around another seven years, and he recovered enough to drag his foot to the toilet with his cane. Her niece said she should put him in a nursing home since it would be bad for the boy to grow up with him half paralyzed; she was only thirty-nine said his niece and could marry again, but she would never leave him, and though the boy couldn't understand the slur of his speech she could converse with him as she did now at the dinner table while the boy listened to the radio in the parlor and his brother was in his club.

It was Friday and the boy could stay up after *Ozzie and Harriet* and *The Life of Riley* and then sleep late the next morning to play in the streets with the neighborhood kids while his brother worked in the ice-cream parlor.

Saturday mornings she did her laundry with the wringer washer her husband had bought when he was flush and it chugged as the blades turned back and forth until she lifted the load with a stick turned white from the bleach; then squeezing it through the rollers she carried it to the window where leaning out from the sill she pinned it on the line from the pulley to the pole in the back yard, the sheets and shirts flapping in the breeze as if they were alive and then smelling fresh from the soap and the breeze when they were dry; and after she spread the sheets over the mattresses she mopped the linoleum and vacuumed the carpet in the parlor where her husband had dragged himself to be out of her way.

She was done by noon and walked to the little shop of the Armenian grocer around the corner whose vegetable baskets lay on the sidewalk and his shop stuffed with jars of spices and the two barrels of green and black olives and the four sizes of bulghur in the bins, the lamb hanging from a hook in the refrigerator closet in the rear from where he carried a leg and shoulder he chopped and sliced for what she would cook in the coming week in her dolmas and kuftahs.

He didn't sell chicken that was costly in those years, but for a special occasion she could choose one in the shop around the other corner where the chicken lady wore a rubber apron and rubber boots and would grab a bird from the cage and slice away the head and plunge the carcass in a barrel of hot water and pluck off the feathers.

Or some Fridays she might buy fresh fish from the shop by the ice-cream parlor, and she could always buy cheese from the shop on the corner whose bins were for the mozzarella of the Italians and what the Armenians would salt and curl with sprinkles of black sesame.

There were also meatless meals with red or green lentils or white beans or chick peas, her cuisine a cross between the Mediterranean and India Asia that she learned since her mother once cooked on an open fire in the vineyard where there was no rain from spring to fall.

On this Saturday evening she cooked a pot of dolma with

the dried baby eggplants she had soaked and then stuffed with rice and the ground lamb and served as always with the fresh bread from the Italian bakery that was on the same street once called *the Dardanelles.*

After dinner she undressed and eased her husband into the tub in the small bathroom where she scrubbed and then toweled him and led him to the bed where the boy helped dress him in his fresh pajamas and lift his paralyzed arm into the sleeve.

Then it was her and the boy's turn in the tub and she held him between her legs as she sat on a little bench and doused him with a pan of warm water from the big pail under the faucets while turning his head when he tried to see between her legs.

He had grown too big for the crib in her bedroom with his father and now slept in a double bed with his brother in the next room, though she would soon need to buy two single beds for them. The stroke had left her husband impotent, yet she loved him no less and held him close as they fell asleep.

She ironed on Sunday mornings and never went to church except for baptisms and weddings. She remembered her father once brought her to a church when they lived in town during the winter rains, and though his face was a blur in her memory she remembered him burying his baby in a graveyard of a church in Damascus after her mother gave birth on the march, and he was buried there himself after he died with his pants soiled from what must have been a kind of dysentery.

Jesus meant little to her, yet she had a deep faith in her personal God who she called *Asdvas Dada* in Armenian, *the Holy Father.* At the same time, she never lost her peasant belief in superstitions, and on this Sunday morning she held her boy's hand and dropped a nickel in his palm to light a candle and ask *Asdvas Dada* to make his father well.

He was old enough now for his brother to lead him the four blocks to the Armenian Orthodox church and show him where to drop the nickel in the brass box under the candles, which he would continue to do every Sunday morning in the years to come, his brother then leading him to his father's nephew who lived a block from the church and had just returned from the army and was an artist who would become the boy's father figure in the years to come.

She returned to the factory on Monday morning, and with her sons in school, her husband would play solitaire or read from the pile of the boy's comic books or sit by the window in the parlor looking down at the avenue. A week ago, he and the boy were on the floor with tears in their eyes waiting for her to come home from work after he must have slipped and fallen and the boy who was home from school was unable to lift him. Hopefully it wouldn't happen again but she could never be sure.

The factory was five blocks away by what used to be called Highpoint Avenue that led to the cliffs above the waterfront and the reservoir with the gulls gliding overhead. It was a small factory with two dozen machines and a trough for the dresses with the pressers behind them sweating in the steam in their sleeveless undershirts. She was not paid by the hour but was a piece-worker and since she was fast she was now earning enough in the post-war boom to afford an RCA Console radio and phonograph so her husband might listen to the Turkish-Armenian records that her son who was his godson would buy in Manhattan as well as the American songs of the Forties and even some classical albums.

Turning seventeen her son had become the man of the house and she depended on him to read official letters and when the wash line broke he climbed the spikes of the pole with a new rope between the pulleys.

Her pay was so good that year she could even afford a summer room for two weeks in an Armenian boarding house in Belmar at the Jersey shore so they could escape the heat in the city, which was so stifling she and the boy would help his father sit on the steps down the three flights of stairs, step by step until he could sit on a chair on the sidewalk between the Chinese laundry man and the Jewish delicatessen.

Then in November 1950 he had a second stroke and she had to sew a plastic sheet for the bed after he couldn't reach the toilet, and she then had to say she was Catholic to the nun at St. Mary's hospital so it would accept him as a charity patient.

It was in Hoboken by a park that was later in a scene in the film *On the Waterfront,* and after a week had passed there was an early snow and so cold her son had to crank his '36 Ford to get it started, and after he drove her and his brother down the viaduct to the charity ward she whispered to the boy to say goodbye to his father, but he didn't know how and just stood at his side touching his hand as they looked at each other and his father's eyes were like pebbles in water.

The Korean War began in the same year and by luck her son was sent to Germany, and when he returned he lived with her and his brother until he married and moved to North Bergen where she and the boy would also move and take the bus to work and school.

Then after he got his photoengraver's union card he was earning enough to move to Ridgewood in the next county, and he would bring her grandchildren who were only a year apart to stay overnight on the weekends. Her younger son who was now in college also came on weekends and after moving to London he would fly back and stay with her in the summer break from his teaching.

But around ten years later photoengraving had been supplanted by a new printing method, and unable to stay in Ridgewood her son moved his family to Fresno in California around the time she was retiring and she could afford a little home near his with her life savings.

Her other son was living in Berkeley by then and he would drive across the valley to spend weekends with her. One morning he had a panic dream where he was searching for his childhood home in West Hoboken as if it were a safe haven, and when he asked her if she missed the old neighborhood she said in English and Armenian: *"Those streets are still wet from my tears."*

In her garden now she had grown a lemon and grapefruit and satsuma and apricot and quince and persimmon and olive trees, plus a green garden of okra and fava beans and tomatoes and zucchini, and along the fence she tied a grapevine not for grapes though they were very sweet small seedless Thompsons, but for the leaves she would harvest when they were young and tender and jar in salt water and wrap around rice and onions in her sarma.

She also had in her front yard a pair of green and purple fig trees and a pomegranate tree whose fruit was not as red and seeds not as hard as sold in market, but was for juice that was so sweet it tasted like ambrosia.

"I am like my father now," she said one morning holding a shovel, though he was only in his thirties when he died on the march and she was now ninety-three. She would go to bed around nine and rise at dawn and sit in her rocking chair sipping her coffee while looking out the wide window at her garden and then work in it until noon when she would eat her main meal, and today it was the purslane her neighbors called weeds that grew between the cracks of the sidewalk and the borders of the lawns.

It was an ancient food and maybe even prehistoric that she sautéed in oil with onions and flavored with lemon juice, and she ate it with the bread she baked herself that was not as crisp as from the old Italian bakery but made with the same kind of dough from unbleached flour.

After a nap she watched her soap called *As the World Turns* whose story she could follow with her limited English. A filmmaker from Berkeley had made a documentary of her own story called *I Will Not Be Sad in This World*, and it would be shown in festivals across the country and abroad.

Then one morning her son called his brother to tell him she was in the hospital after she broke her hip and a surgeon inserted a screw in it. Her neighbor across the cul-de-sac was laying bricks in his front yard, and after she asked for some cement to plug the hole in her stucco to keep away the ants, she fell on the pavement losing her balance when her wheelbarrow overturned.

"She needed that cement like a hole in her head," her son said to his brother. She had been a queen of cleanliness since she was a girl, but the ants won the final battle.

She could hobble with a walker after she recovered, and they hired a friendly middle-aged Armenian immigrant woman from Yerevan who cooked and cleaned while she sat in her garage that had become her second living room with a rug and a second rocking chair, and with the door open she tossed crumbs to the flock of sparrows that would peck in the driveway while the neighborhood kids rode their bikes around the cul-de-sac.

But one day when the caretaker couldn't come she was left alone due to a mix-up in the phone calls and her son in Berkeley called his niece who found her on the floor in the bathroom with her skirt soaked in urine after she tried to use the toilet by herself.

She had a minor heart-attack, said the intern in the hospital, and it was the beginning of her decline. A while later when her son came from Berkeley for the weekend he found her smeared with her diarrhea after she had tried to rise to the toilet near her bed, and he learned how her father died when he was cleaning her.

In her story of the march she had said only that he got sick in Damascus and was buried there, and as he was wiping the diarrhea from her thighs she looked up at him between her legs and said this was how her father died and he finally knew what sick really meant.

Her sons and the caretaker did the best they could in changing her diaper and swabbing her bedsores with cotton Q-tips, but she would be left alone at night until she was finally approved for Medi-Cal and her son found a decent nursing home near his where he would come every morning and his brother would come on the weekends and sit at her side drawing her face.

She was in a room with two others and when she first arrived she was in a bed by the corridor, but her son from Berkeley had her moved by the window after the woman there had died, more for himself than her since she was beyond caring by then, and as he sat drawing her she would look out the window at the little plum tree that would blossom and then turn bare in the passing seasons as the world turned, her wrinkles deepening like the map of her life across the century from the death march to her rest home.

Her mind was clear at first, but after who knew how many mini-strokes it would mix memory and imagination like a dream and she would lie peacefully except when wincing with pain from her hemorrhoids.

Nor did she ever complain, said one of her nurse's aides, a

nineteen-year old Cambodian beauty like a Khmer princess who changed her diaper and dropped the old one in the bin.

She lay there for six years from the beginning of the new century to when she was turning a hundred and one, her body shriveling year by year until she was only skin and bones as if she were returning to the earth. She could only guess the year of her birth but it must have been in March since she remembered her mother once said in Turkish that she was a wild child because she had been a March Baby, and it was in March when she died.

He wanted to be at her side but he couldn't keep sitting there, and his brother called a few days later saying she passed away alone in the middle of the night before the nurse's aide came in the morning and found her body cold and inert.

She was the afterword of Freud's *Das Unbehagen in der Kultur*. She was of the good-natured and the un-neurotic that would inherit the earth and hopefully save it. She was what Freud thought might face the challenge of those who make bombs and wars. There had always been millions like her and would be millions more.

After the Massacre

One day when she was visiting a friend from the orphanage who was on her way to be married in America, an older woman in a room next door named Annah was also on her way there to join her son and asked her to come and marry him.

She knew of other picture brides going to America, and not wanting to remain a servant she agreed. Her master's mother, who was kind to her in the two years she worked for them and who had taught her how to wear a cloth in her first menstruation, was sad to lose her and gifted her with gold coins before she was to leave; then as if these coins were her dowry, Annah bought with them a ring for her son and a cheaper one for her.

Her name Zaruhi was from the word for gold and in her submission the loss of the coins would be like an omen in the years ahead. She had lost her mother on the march and had needed her since then, yet Annah would not be a mother but a mother-in-law.

Annah herself had been an orphan who was adopted by her uncle Petros and was the same age as his two boys from his late wife, and she lived with them and his daughters from his second wife until she married; then Petros' youngest son Armenag was born in the same year as Annah's son Vahan, and Vahan and Armenag would each escape the Turkish draft and flee to America where Armenag would be Vahan's best man when the young Zaruhi arrived.

She had just turned sixteen and it was a gloomy marriage that was not in a church since it was during lent, and she had no wedding dress and even had to borrow a pair of shoes, which made her feel so ashamed she would borrow a wedding gown a year later and then pose for a photograph as if she had a proper marriage like her friends.

Nor did she sleep with Vahan for several weeks until she could finally "*close her eyes and let it happen;*" yet he did respect her and desired her sexually, and though he was thirteen years older, he had fine features and a strong character and she would get used to him until she could have a child.

He worked for a dry cleaner and she started sewing in a factory, and they moved to an apartment in West Hoboken on Highpoint Avenue where Annah would distill fermented raisins in the bathtub during the years of Prohibition that had just begun.

She was disgusted by the stink and complained saying she handed Annah her pay each week and didn't need the money, but Annah enjoyed selling her *araq* that made her popular. They lived above a Turkish bath that was for women on Fridays and men on Saturday nights, and the patrons would come upstairs for Annah's bootleg that would annoy the young Zaruhi even more as if she were living in a saloon.

Yet she was still too young and submissive to rebel. She worked all day while Annah cooked and cared for the apartment, and after dinner Vahan would go to one of the cafes in the Dardanelles while she sat with Annah in the kitchen on the couch by the coal stove where Annah would tell of her life back in Tigranagert before the massacre.

It was an ancient city on a mesa above the banks of the Tigris founded by King Tigranes that was later named Diyarbekir after it was conquered by Bekir the Turk, and the Armenian quarter mixed with those of the Turks and Assyrians and Kurds, and the home of Annah's uncle Petros was built around a courtyard with the same black stone as the rest of the city.

He was a *najar* that was an ancient Mesopotamian word for carpenter still used not only in Turkish but in Persian and Arabic and the other tongues of the middle and near east, and when last names were formed his became Najar-yan, the *yan* for family, and his oldest sons Boghos and Garabed became an architect and a master builder around whom Annah would weave her story with the rest of the family, the young Zaruhi listening as if it were replacing the family she lost on the march, especially after she fell in love with the youngest son Armenag who was her husband's best man and Annah's first cousin.

Armenag lived with his older sister Vartanush who when he was seventeen had sold her prized embroidery to pay for their escape to join his other older sister Nevart, who had married her husband Ohannes in West Hoboken after he too escaped the draft.

Unable to live in Nevart's small apartment, Vartanush married another escapee, Hagop, who happened to be a cousin of Annah on her mother's side that made their families even closer.

Vartanush, whose name meant sweet rose, was really a sweet woman, and the young Zaruhi loved her while she loved her brother Armenag. Vartanush's son was seven and her baby daughter a year old when Annah and Zaruhi moved to Highpoint Avenue, and their families were often together, but Zaruhi's love for Armenag was always from a distance and only with her *"eyes,"* as she would later say.

In the meantime, Annah's story turned to when she and Zaruhi were brought to America by Arsen, who was not only Annah's relative on her mother's side, but whose sister Arpi was the wife of Annah's cousin Garabed, and after Garabed and Boghos were executed as resistance leaders, Arpi was rescued from the massacre by a Kurdish neighbor who made her his wife.

Arsen and his brother Levon had escaped to America where Arsen became a soldier in the American army in the World War, and after the war he went to Beirut to find a wife and another for his brother and he wanted to continue to Diyarbekir for his sister Arpi until Annah told him it was impossible.

Annah had survived the massacre after her husband died and she had made her way to Beirut as a washer woman in the following years, and when Arsen arranged the visas he declared her his mother and Zaruhi his sister and also as his sister the wife for his brother who happened to be one of Zaruhi's friends from the orphanage.

Back in the massacre when Boghos was executed with his brother Garabed, his wife Zabel was left for dead by the mercenary Chechens who took their daughters Manushag and Astghig as slaves in their nomadic tribe, and the girls lived with these Chechens until Zabel, who didn't die but was only knocked unconscious, found one of little Manushag's notes.

Boghos had taught Manushag how to read and write, and she would hand her secret notes of her location to itinerant merchants who would take them to the city, and after Zabel found one of these notes she paid the Chechens to get her daughters back, and on their way to Alexandria where Zabel had relatives she asked Garabed's widow Arpi to come with them, but Arpi had children with the Kurd by then, and years later Arsen and Levon would weep when Manushag came to America and told them how they lost their sister who stayed behind and was lost forever.

Manushag and her sister and mother lived in Alexandria until she wrote to her uncle Armenag in West Hoboken where he had been raising Vartanush's children while their father Hagop was unemployed, and when Armenag didn't have enough for Manushag's passage, he asked Annah for a loan, and Annah would reach into her petticoat to give him the pay the young Zaruhi handed her each week, so it was actually Zaruhi who brought Manushag to America, and they were the same age and would become like sisters.

But Manushag, whose name meant violet, had yet to arrive when the young Zaruhi listened to Annah's story by the coal stove in the cold winter nights when the door of the back room would be shut to store the big ceramic jar of pickled cabbage and baby eggplants and the other jar of the cold chunks of lamb and congealed white fat, Annah narrating not only the story of the Najarian family but of others from Diyarbekir who had come to West Hoboken along with the refugees from other Turkish cities after the genocide, the massacres always in the background with swords like those that sliced the throats of uncles like Boghos and Garabed and the rape and slaughter of aunts like their teen-age sister who had long red hair, every family bearing bones in their closets too painful to remember or forget.

Near Highpoint Avenue a few blocks from the Dardanelles was the building called Swiss Turn Hall from the Turnveirein gymnastics of the Swiss Germans, and the Armenians would rent the hall for their theatre when Armenag, who in his late twenties was a prompter in the hood in the middle of the stage when he asked the teenage Zaruhi to play a small part as a cham-bermaid in one of the melodramas, and the love between their eyes was like Annah's story about Ohan back in Diyarberkir.

Ohan had also been in love with his cousin's wife and he had fled to America when she was pregnant with his child, and when the wife came to West Hoboken after her husband died, Ohan supported her family, one of whom was his son, with his work as a laborer.

Armenag's jewelry sold so well in these years that he moved Vartanush and his nephew Ashod and niece Armen to a nicer home in the next town of West New York where his other sister Nevart and her two boys had moved when her husband Ohannes was earning good money as a photoengraver, and when Manushag arrived she moved there with her new husband whose name was also Vahan who had fought the Turks with the Armenian Legion of the French Army.

Vartanush's son Ashod, Arthur in English and Archie to his pals, and Nevart's son Garabed, named for Garabed who was killed, Charles in English and Charlie to his pals, were both precocious artists when they were boys, and Armenag was talented not only in his jewelry but in drawing as well, and Zaruhi would ride the trolley from Highpoint Avenue to visit them in West New York whenever she could.

She worked all week, yet her Sundays and holidays would be filled with picnics and feasts for the rest of the decade while there was always plenty to eat.

She was twenty-five by then, and unable to conceive she went to a doctor who opened somewhere inside her that was blocked, and nine months later she lay in her bedroom in terrible pain all day and night while Annah was in the kitchen and the iceman carried his chunk of ice with the burlap on his shoulder and the customers came for their bottles of *araq,* the baby finally arriving in a healthy nine pounds and his umbilical cord buried in the back yard so he would always be tied to the earth and never know loneliness.

It was in December after the Great Crash and the beginning of the Depression, and she nursed him for two years while she returned to the factory that was around the corner where Annah would bring him to her breast.

The sweet Vartanush whom everyone loved was now suffering from colon cancer and she wore a sac at her side when Zaruhi brought her baby to show him to her, Armenag out of work and his face drawn from worry and grief while the teenage Ashod was the sole support of their home with his job as a clerk.

Meanwhile Zaruhi's fights with Vahan had grown so fierce she wouldn't have sex with him and their marriage would soon end; she was no longer a girl but a woman and no longer under Annah's control.

Vartanush died and Hagop and Ashod and Armen moved back to West Hoboken, and when the destitute Armenag had nowhere to go he went to Zaruhi's factory where she took off the ring he had made for her when he was flush, and he found a room in West Hoboken as well.

She was leaving Vahan, she said to him, regardless of whether he would marry her or not, and there was nothing he could say.

Her boy Tomas turned out to be so much like her there seemed no trace of Vahan, yet Annah and his father adored him, and it was unthinkable to separate them. He was four when they all had moved from Highpoint Avenue to an apartment by Bergenline Avenue, and when Zaruhi decided to leave she moved with her Tomas two blocks from them in a building on the Avenue owned by an Italian who welcomed her.

Years earlier she had worked for an Armenian whose son Yesnik was her age and he married her friend Anahid when he became a lawyer, and they had been good friends when she asked Yesnik for help with her divorce.

Back one day when she was a servant girl in Beirut, she was delivering a can of lunch to her master in town when an old Armenian man called to her from the street and asked her name so he could send it to an exchange where survivors could find each other, and she told the old man she didn't know her last name but she was from Adana and she remembered her cousin Arshag on her father's side who was her older brother's age, and the old man sent her name *Zaruhi* and *Adana* and *Arshag* to the exchange, and a while later a letter came from Arshag to her master's home saying she should wait there for him to come and get her, but it was too late since she was already going to America with Annah.

Alas, replied Arshag, he would never see her again, yet he

told her that in America was her mother's first cousin Petros who lived in Binghamton, New York, and she would eventually find him there whom she would call her uncle.

He lived on a farm with his wife and seven children, and after Yesnik began the divorce she paid the rent to her Italian landlord and took Tomas on the train to Binghamton where they stayed the summer with who had become by then her new family.

Then in September she pleaded with the principal to admit her little Tomas in the school around the corner though he wouldn't be five until December, and he would wait for her after school in the little movie theater up the street until she came home from work, and in time he would see his father and grand-mother who lived by the school.

Yesnik said she mustn't be seen with anyone for two years until the court appearance, but Armenag had rented a room near her, and she did see him there secretly.

Then one day came old Ohan offering to help her.

He was in his seventies by then, yet still so healthy he was known to walk for miles to save the nickel trolley fare, and having become like an old hayseed so thrifty and indifferent to his dress he was nicknamed Cockroach *Om-mo*, the word for uncle since he was actually a cousin of the old Petros of the Najarian family.

Yet he was a kind old man who wouldn't hurt a fly, and see-ing the single mother Zaruhi who had always been fond of him and was now alone with her boy, he offered to help her with the rent and to look out for her, and when he first came for dinner and started to crumble in her soup the stale bread he brought in his pocket, she told him to put it back and served him her fresh bread from the Italian bakery.

He slept on a quilt on the floor and was out in the morning walking wherever it was he would save the nickel trolley fare, and she was happy to see how happy he was to have found a home after he had lived alone for so long, until one day Manushag's husband Vahan came and said:

"Zaruhi, why is Cockroach living here? If you need money I can help you."

No, she said, he was only looking out for her, and Vahan said

Annah was spreading the rumor that she was sleeping with him, so the humble Ohan had to leave and return to living alone.

She had always known how devoted Annah was to her son for whom she had once bought a ring with the gold coins and only a cheaper one for his bride to be, and having lived with her ex-mother-in-law for twelve years the ex-daughter in law Zaruhi knew how far and wide Annah's gossip would spread as if it were a kind of vengeance; yet Yesnik would soon succeed with the divorce and she and Armenag could finally wed.

It would be in Manushag's new home in North Bergen that was only a short ride away, and it was on Manushag's birthday that was the same as George Washington's, and Manushag wanted her "Little Aram" to be the best man though he was only five, and Armenag's sister Nevart's son called "Big Aram" was a first rate violinist and he played with the family friend Vartan who was a professional oud player and Manushag's Vahan played his clarinet, and there was much merriment with song and dance all day and evening.

But alas, Armenag's nephew Ashod and niece Armen couldn't come because their father Hagop stayed loyal to his cousin Annah, and the eight-year old Tomas who was now Tommy to his pals was the only one who could breach the divide between their families.

He had turned out to be a good-natured boy who blended in with everyone, and Armenag became a second father to him who was actually his godfather and took him to the World Fair in Queens that would be one of the most treasured memories of the little Tommy's childhood.

He was ten by then and his mother was pregnant, and she cried worrying about him when she and Armenag had to leave him alone on the train to Binghamton, yet he waved happily through the window while he sat like an adult as the train pulled away on the tracks in Weehawken up the Palisades along the river.

And when he returned at the end of August his baby brother was named Petros after Armenag's father, yet Tommy would call him "Pete" like the Petros in Binghamton whom he called "Uncle Pete."

Once again Zaruhi's second child was so much like her there seemed no trace of Armenag, and her two boys looked so alike they were like full brothers and not half, but as the little Pete grew up he would question her about Tommy's other family.

And it was around then that she and Annah met at a banquet in Swiss Turn Hall one day, and she cried as she said that Annah finally had her revenge in regard to Armenag's stroke, and the old Annah, who was in her eighties by then, said softly:

"I didn't want revenge, my daughter."

Yes, the young Zaruhi had been in fact like her daughter when Vahan was once so sick he was suspected of having T.B. and the doctor said he had to be isolated, so Annah took her daughter-in-law on the train to California until he could recover.

Annah's oldest son Karnig had settled in Los Angeles with his wife Araxi, and Annah and the eighteen-year old Zaruhi lived with them in what for Zaruhi would be the time of her life while Annah had her hands full keeping the young suitors at bay.

Hollywood had become the center of the world by then, and Araxi and her friends would treat the vivacious young ingenue to party after party where they would pose like Flapper Girls in their incessant photographs, and from then on California would always seem like a Shangri-La to the star struck young Zaruhi, and her uncle Petros in Binghamton would later move there to Pasadena when he retired.

It was Annah who had taken her to California, the same Annah of the stinking raisins and the petticoat stuffed with her pay, the Annah who took her gold away and was as devoted to her Vahan as she would later be to her Tommy and Pete, the Annah who was not like a mother yet would treat her like a daughter despite the girl's ambivalent feelings.

Vahan didn't really have T.B. and the trouble in his lungs were instead from his heavy smoking, and when she returned to the factory and Annah to her bootleg, Annah, who seemed to know every Armenian in every city, would take the young Zaruhi on her off days like a daughter to visit friends all the way to Paterson by trolley and to Watertown in Massachusetts by ferry, and the years passed until the baby Tomas was born.

Annah died after the last meeting in Swiss Turn Hall, and though Zaruhi wouldn't go to the funeral, the old bard would loom in her memories for the rest of her life.

The Korean War began after Annah died and then Armenag also died, and after Tommy was drafted she asked his friend Bela to help her and little Pete take the bus from Jersey City to Camp Kilmer from where Tommy would be sent away.

Meanwhile her ex-husband Vahan was driven there separately by a friend, and after they each said their separate goodbyes, they went together to a Howard Johnson motel restaurant where they sat around a big table and Vahan paid for their sandwiches and desserts.

She hadn't seen her ex-husband in the sixteen years since the divorce, and they didn't speak to each other while Bela and the friend carried on the conversation, and the little Pete looked at his mother and then at his brother's father wondering what they were thinking, the silence between them dissolving in the blur of his memory except for the *"club sandwich"* he had never heard of, which was a stack of triple slices of toast with bacon, lettuce and tomato whose taste he would never forget.

Vahan died of a heart attack while Tommy was in Germany, and she went to view the casket in the funeral parlor in her son's place since he couldn't fly back, and she would later say that she felt the ghost of the corpse would rise and start fighting with her again.

Yes, she would say, she had always felt guilty for taking her son away from his father, yet she would make up for it as best she could, and she hosted in her parlor the meal that was forty days after the funeral called the *hoki josh*, the dinner for the soul, which was for Vahan's friends whom she had known but not seen since the divorce, while the little Pete who had just entered puberty sat on the couch in the kitchen reading his comic books and stuffing himself with her lulu kebab and pilaf.

Tommy married and moved away after he returned from Germany, and after her Pete left for college she was only fifty-three when Manushag wanted to fix her up with a well-to-do widower, but she had enough of husbands and said she had always been able to take care of herself.

She had moved near Manushag in North Bergen, and since Annah and Vahan had died, she could once again visit Armenag's nephew Ashod and niece Armen whom she had known since they were children; and though Ashod, whom Pete called Archie, lived half the year in Woodstock where he had become a painter, he returned in the fall and winter.

Ashod was only seven when she and Annah came from Ellis Island and stayed with Vartanush until they could find a place of their own, and when they first came into the kitchen Vartanush said of her little Ashod who was drawing on the porcelain table top:

"There he goes again, making his little snakes."

And the young Zaruhi would be fond of him from then on. And when his sister Armen was a little girl she once sewed a dress for her that Armen would remember for the rest of her life.

Meanwhile Ashod's cousin Charlie had become so successful as an illustrator, he hired an architect to build a home in Tenafly that was all woods in those years, and Charlie's wife Edna was so fond of his aunt Zaruhi that she would often be invited there, especially when Edna was giving birth in the hospital and she stayed in Tenafly caring for little Craig while Charlie was working.

In the meantime, the little daughter of Manushag's son Aram was the same age as Tommy's toddlers, and Tommy and Aram brought them for her to babysit on the weekends.

And so passed the years of her family togetherness until she followed Tommy to Fresno, and several years later she flew back to see everyone and stayed with Ashod and Armen who had moved to a little bungalow in Long Island after their father Hagop died.

Back when Ashod was painting half the year in Woodstock and the other half in West Hoboken, she had told him his work was too dark and he should brighten it. She had a good eye and he respected it. Her older brother was a precocious artist before he disappeared on the march, and she had inherited the same genes for art that she had passed on to Tommy who was also talented as a child and was ambidextrous like Archie and

Armenag that added to Manushag wanting to believe he was really Armenag's son, which angered Zaruhi though she understood it was because Manushag was so fond of Tommy.

Ashod no longer painted in Woodstock, yet his paintings did indeed brighten, and he had stacks of them in the dirt floor garage by the bungalow. She stayed there a week and then of course visited with Manushag and Charlie and Edna and her dear friends. She was blessed with a friendly nature and she loved people who loved her in return.

Then back in Fresno she continued to see her old friend, Zimruth, whom she had known from West Hoboken and who had settled in Fresno with her husband Yerem and now lived alone in her old age on the other side of town where Zaruhi would ride the bus to see her, and when Pete came on weekends he would often drive her there and get to know Zimruth herself whose name meant emerald.

Zimruth had been raped by a gang of Turks during the massacre when she was a girl and she would never be able to bear children afterwards, and Pete used what his mother had told him about her in his novel where he created a chorus he called the Daughters of Memory as if Zimruth was one of them.

Just as Annah once narrated her history of families to the young Zaruhi in the coal stove apartment on Highpoint Avenue, so too did the old Zaruhi now tell her own version to her Pete with her own talent for storytelling in which she turned Annah's memories into her own saga like an old bard improvising on an ancient theme.

She of course never knew the paterfamilias Petros and his family, yet she could imagine him by his old photo with his walrus mustache that Armenag had enlarged and framed and now hung on the wall by her bed.

The first wife of Petros was from an educated protestant family in the missionary college city of Kharpet that was north of Diyarbekir, and though it was unknown how she came to marry Petros, she had brought her Bible, and after she died when her boys were still children the Bible was later given to her second son Garabed when he married Arpi, and Arpi kept it when she was saved by her Kurdish neighbor, and when Arpi couldn't go to Alexandria with Boghos' widow Zabel, she gave the Bible to Zabel, and Zabel's daughter Manushag later brought it to America where Manushag once told little Pete it would go to him since he was the last Najarian. But after Manushag died it stayed with her son, Little Aram, whose last name was that of his father Vahan.

Both Manushag and Vahan were long gone by the time Zaruhi became the bard of the Najarian chronicle, and she had broken her hip when Ashod died and Pete had gone back to Long Island to salvage his beloved Archie's paintings in the dirt floor garage.

Several years passed while Pete tried to promote the paintings for Archie's sake, and his mother Zaruhi was in the nursing home when he learned that his cousin Aram had stolen them from him.

Little Aram didn't really want the paintings that he thought were worthless, but he got involved in the theft with his wife Lillian, whose Armenian name was Shushanig, and their greed led to their betrayal.

It was another family story that Pete would publish in his book, *The Paintings of Art Pinajian,* and it would end with the family Bible that Manushag said would go to him as the last Najarian.

He loved who he called his "Auntie Manushag," though she was really his first cousin, and his first memory of her was when she held him naked between her legs in the bathtub like his mother would, and her body was soft with big breasts and her hair was reddish and she had a beautiful face like a movie star's.

She was like his second mother and his mother had brought him to her home in North Bergen when his school where he was in first grade was snowbound and closed, and he slept in one of the double beds in the room with her sister, his Auntie Astghig who was crippled by a car accident when she came from Alexandria and she had to walk with crutches, and she too had a beautiful face.

His cousin Aram had his own room next to Auntie Astghig, and he was not only like an older brother but was his godfather who was only eight when Uncle Vahan had to stand behind him and hold his arms at the baptism.

He loved his cousin Aram and would sneak into his room and try to wear his baseball glove that was too big for his small fingers, and Aram would treat him like his little brother.

And on Thanksgiving of that same year Uncle Vahan drove his paralyzed father to the dinner and Auntie Manushag sat her beloved Uncle Armenag at the head of the table in the dining room, and Tommy and Aram came from the football game of their rival high-schools, and little Pete would remember this grand event for the rest of his life as if everyone were his family.

But they were all gone except Aram when Pete asked him over the phone to send him the Bible, and Aram said no.

"You have no children," he said, and he said he was going to leave it to his daughter who had four children.

Yet she had married an Irishman and her children were growing up Irish and the Bible would lie in the closet with the fly leaf of the names and birthdates written in an illegible Armenian script none of their Irish family could read, and Pete would never see the Bible or Little Aram again.

Such was the end of Pete's story about the end of the

Armenag and Zaruhi with Archie and Armen

To Ellen Pinsky

Dear Ellen,

I was flabbergasted when I saw your name listed on the cover of Threepenny Review, and after reading your piece I was even more amazed to learn that you had become a psychoanalyst!

We haven't been friends for more than thirty years, and yet I never forget when I first met you with Robert in Alan Cheuse's pad on Prosper Street where your eyes were so beautiful they grabbed me like a vision.

Robert, who was called Bob before he changed it, had just met you himself a few months earlier, and he was on his way to a summer program in Spain and you replied to my postcard to your summer camp thanking me for my friendship in your love for him.

You were turning eighteen while he and I would be twenty, and after I moved to Neilson Street in the following semester he was in a fraternity house and you in a dorm at Douglas, and he asked me to stay out one day so he could sleep with you in my bed for your first sex together, and I later went to your wedding during the winter break.

Then married, you lived off campus in your own flat on Easton Avenue where you cooked a delicious meal with pork-chops for us one night, and when Robert got the fellowship to Stanford I drove to Manhattan to say bon voyage and you were crashing with Bob Maniquis and his wife Pam in their flat by Columbia where you and Pam were asleep while I listened to Bob and Robert talking all night, and I didn't see you again until the following spring when my friend Gregory and I drove out west and I visited you for a week in Palo Alto while Gregory stayed in Berkeley.

I visited again the next year before I was to leave for London, and it was in those two visits that I got to know how smart you really were when we chatted while Robert was in class, and you gave me a copy of Ford Madox Ford's *The Good Soldier* that was new to me and especially *Flaubert's Three Tales* that would be one of the monuments of my writing life.

Like Robert you were much smarter than I and I looked up to your intelligence as I did to his, yet I never got to chat with you again, even when you both came for a year in London and you lived in affluent Chiswick while I was in a flat in Spitalfields that Robert called *"squalid,"* and I would crash on your couch after the tubes stopped running, and one morning you made a *matzo brei* for breakfast that was so delicious I can still taste it.

How beautiful you were and how afraid I was of you when you were so quiet while I would talk with Robert as if I knew what I was talking about, yet I never talked to you as if you would know how full of crap I really was.

My sickness had become so virulent by then I was headed for a breakdown, yet you were not aware of this and never would be. I had been sick since I was a child, always feeling inferior to friends like Robert and afraid of women like you, which was at the root of why I would never marry and would live alone for most of my life.

And so passed that year in London when we sat so close in the concerts and theatres and yet were so far apart, and I didn't see you again for two years while Robert was teaching in Chicago where your first daughter was born, and I mailed you a baby blanket from Liberty's in London that was woven in a Scotch plaid pattern with soft Scottish mohair like you were so soft and lovely in my memory of you.

Then you both came east to visit your parents, and one night you stopped to see me in Manhattan where I was staying with Beate who I had known since I had known you and who had the same kind of beautiful eyes as yours, and when I came out to the street by your car you told me I should take her with me to California and not wait for her husband to return from his trip.

I couldn't do that to him, I said, he was like a brother to me, and you said he wouldn't be a brother to me anymore, and though you had spoken with Beate for only a few minutes, you knew what she was feeling as if you were sisters while I was blind as if I didn't know her at all.

I didn't see you again until after my breakdown when Robert was teaching in Wellesley and your second daughter was born, and I drove across country to visit while you were so busy with your daughters I was afraid to be in your way, and I would walk in the autumn leaves where I would hide my crying.

Your third daughter was born around five years later while another breakdown had led me to a Reichian therapist who helped tie my crying to the autonomic nervous system, which was what Reichian therapy was really all about and which later led to my involuntary movements in my Vipassana practice where I would breathe into them for the rest of my life.

You of course knew nothing of this, and I didn't see you again for four more years until I came east from where I was living in Detroit when I would again keep out of your way while going to the Fine Arts in Boston and chatting only with Robert in the evenings, except for one evening when he asked me to watch the kids so he could take you out to celebrate your anniversary.

I wanted to visit again during the following winter break, but Robert mailed me a postcard saying sorry he would be too busy, and though it was true he was busier than ever after his new book of criticism led him to friends much smarter and more important to him than I, I had thought of him as family since we were freshmen in college, and I felt he ws now telling me our friendship had passed and he had outgrown it.

He was polite and would reply to my notes when I tried to keep in touch, but I didn't see either of you again for another five years until you settled in Berkeley where he became a full professor and had no time for me, and you were further away than ever before.

I was in bad shape by then, scraping by with part-time jobs and feeling that my writing had come to nothing, yet it was around then I felt saved by learning how to paint, and one evening when Robert invited me to the dinner he gave for Alan who was visiting from back east, I brought a few paintings to show you while you were in the kitchen preparing another of your delicious meals, and though you were polite you didn't say what you thought of them.

Then one day we met by chance at the green grocer on the corner of Shattuck Avenue and Vine Street where you came to shop, and you paused in your busy life to chat with me as we once did years before when you gave me the Flaubert book.

It was a morning when you weren't teaching and you shared with me how much you enjoyed driving over the bay across the Richmond Bridge to your school in Marin, and as I looked into your beautiful eyes I was not afraid of you anymore, and I wanted to hug you with how much I've always loved you since the day I met you when you were just a girl.

Yes, I wanted to say, I knew exactly how you felt; I too loved driving over the bay and we always had so much in common that had been buried in my fear of you, and yet in all the years we had known each other I had never hugged you and I was still afraid of reaching across the zucchini and eggplants to even kiss your cheek like the French would do, and the moment fled like a spot of time that would never happen again.

Nor did I speak with you again until Robert decided to move back east to teach in Boston and you had a going away party in your back yard.

It happened to be on the same day I went to a memorial for a friend's child who had drowned, and I was very shaken by the casket in their home when I arrived at your party, and you had paused for a moment from hosting it and were resting on a bench on your deck, and I sat next to you wanting to share how shaken I was by the memorial as if you were a kind of sister like you seemed at the green grocer's, and I said:

"You've always meant so much to me, Ellen."

And you turned to me with your beautiful eyes and said with a coldness that was like a knife in my heart:

"But you weren't nice to me, Peter."

And called back to the party, you stood up and turned away, never to see me or care to see me for the rest of your life.

How could you have been so warm at the green grocer and then so cold, as if you were what was called bipolar? How and when was I not nice to you? Was it when I would speak only to Robert and never to you?

I had a history of seeking love from those who would turn away; it was part of my sickness and like a mirror of my own coldness that would close the valves of my heart like stone. How could I love you or anyone when I was so desperate for love myself?

And the years would pass when I mailed you letters like this, always hoping you would answer; nor would Robert reply again when I tried to keep in touch.

I asked our mutual friend Bob Hass about why, and Bob said he was apparently angry at me, but angry at what? Of all his friends I was the one who had loved him the most, like in that summer in Long Branch when I watched him read *Ulysses* without a guide and then the eight Modern Library volumes of *Remembrance of Things Past* while passing the optician exam to please his beloved optician father.

I didn't have his genius but I had the same devotion to writing when he wrote to me how happy he was with you in the first year of your marriage, and I would save his letters until years later when I would send them to him as if to say how close we had been, and yet when I wanted them back because of how much they meant me to me, his postcard said they were legally his, as if he didn't trust I would keep them private.

What was it about me that would make those whose love I needed turn away? Twenty years passed and I mailed you both a copy of my book about my mother, and after neither of you responded, I wasn't going to mail you the second of my trilogy that was about my cousin Archie, but Bob said I should, and when there was no response a second time, I didn't mail you the third that included how important you both were in my life.

And now here is your own book that I just discovered after reading your piece in Threepenny Review.

You titled it: *Death and Fallibility in the Psychoanalytic Encounter: Mortal Gifts*, and while it is as brilliant as I expected from knowing how brilliant you have always been, it is for me about much more than what your title says; it is really about your love for psychoanalysis and for Freud who invented it. You love it like my surgeon loved surgery when he sliced open my belly and snipped away the tumor in my ureter.

He was a sweet guy like you were sweet, and I got to know

him in my office visits and how he loved his work like Norik my mechanic loved to work on cars because he loved cars; and when I gave him one of my books he told me he also loved to write like you love to write, and he would go back to his writing after he retired and moved to Paradise Valley near Yellowstone where I would visit my late writer friend Gatz Hjortsberg and his wife Marian.

Yes, you always loved writing, and you weave into your narrative your same love of poesy that you once shared in our youth when you gave me your copies of *The Good Soldier* and Flaubert's *Three Tales.*

I've read your book twice now and I renewed it on link at the library. I wish I could buy it but it costs forty dollars even in paper and I still live on the edge. I read it greedily in search of who you have become in the past thirty years since I had seen you, but alas there is so little that is personal, except for a dream you once had and your emotional memory of your late analyst.

It is a kind of history of psychoanalysis from your reading of Freud's early papers and those of his followers, yet I'm more curious about how and why you chose it when it was so expensive and took so long. You were in it for four years before you began your training that must have been after your daughters were grown, and I imagine it was not only for therapy but for how fascinating it was, as if it were a kind of drama like what my old teacher Francis Fergusson once called in his study of the *Purgatorio: Dante's Drama of the Mind.*

Yet the mind is only part of what makes us human, which is tied to the other part that makes us cry. I imagine you cried in your therapy sessions and your analysands may have cried in your sessions with them, and though crying may be induced by the mind, it comes from a deeper part.

Actors can simulate crying and maybe even actually cry like the actor Jack Nicolson in the film *Five Easy Pieces* in 1970 when we had the same Reichian Therapist who had his sessions in Los Angeles as well as in San Francisco.

His name was Phil Curcuruto and he was my mother's age and from a family of Sicilian immigrants in the Lower East Side, and he had become a successful chiropractor when he learned of Reich with Ellsworth Baker, who was Reich's student and colleague.

Reich himself had been a student and colleague of Freud until he discovered his breathing technique, and Curcuruto via Baker would practice it in its orthodox form before it branched into what would be called bioenergetics.

My friend and mentor Willy Smolak, who Robert knew from Rutgers, had been a client of Phil's and recommended him to me in the spring of 1970 when I was falling apart in my breakdown, which was when Phil's other client "Jack" finished *Five Easy Pieces* that I happened to see in a preview in the American Film Institute when I was visiting my friend Jim Kitses who was teaching there. If I'm not mistaken, you and Robert met Kitses with me in London when Jim and I were at the British Film Institute.

It's a good film and Jack's character cries while sitting by his father who was paralyzed by a stroke like my father when I was a toddler. My first novel *Voyages* that was rooted in my father's stroke was published in 1971 when I was still seeing Phil, and Phil asked for a copy to give to Jack in L.A. in case it could connect me to Hollywood, which of course would be impossible since I had no talent for such a connection.

The technique that Phil used with me and with Jack was very simple and yet very profound, and contrary to what Freud called the "talking cure," there was no talking except in his guiding me in how to exhale and hyperventilate, as if he were what he liked to call himself: "a witch doctor," which really meant shaman.

It was in fact related to the breathing practices since prehistory with other names such as *chi* or *shakti* or whatever it was called in jungles or monasteries, though Reich was the first in the west to show how it was manifest in the orgasm and the primal scream and how the knots in our armor would impede its flow.

My first and most important orgasm was at the dawn of my puberty in a wet dream when I was turning eleven where a visionary girl embraced me in the flash of light and the ooze through my penis, and I woke stunned and stupefied until I could stagger to the bathroom while my mother changed the sheet and lay a cloth under a fresh one so the mattress wouldn't be stained the next time.

There would be stains on that cloth in the following years but never such an overwhelming revelation that I would be seeking for the rest of my life, as if every fiber of me had unraveled into the light itself that kept expanding until there was no me at all.

But in the blaze of adolescence and the heat of passion in the rest of my life there would no visionary girl like Dante's Beatrice, and instead there would be what we called sex that would drive our lives always seeking in the orgasm that could find her as when I lay with Bernie in the spring of 1967 in her bedroom in Waterloo while deep inside her I looked down at her sobbing in an ecstasy I could only imagine as if she were gone, gone beyond, gone utterly beyond.

She was only thirty then, as delicate as a dove and yet as fierce as a revolutionary, who twenty years later would save the South Bank from development and a park would be named for her after she killed herself in a forest in Scotland, the how and why she killed herself the contrary of her sobbing in that afternoon that I would not know until I would sob after my primal scream that came from the same realm deep inside us that is beyond words or image.

What was the sobbing and the letting go of my sickness if only for a nanosecond?

I'm not asking you of course, nor is there anywhere in your book or in Freud or the mind itself that can be expressed in words where the sobbing really comes from, and this letter is no longer to you but to whom I've been speaking since I was child asking the mystery behind the candles to make my father well again.

There was never an answer of course, nor will you ever answer, you of the beautiful eyes who said I was not nice to you and later fell in love with psychoanalysis.

Yet what is the psyche and what is its sickness not only mine but in Freud's *Das Unbehagen in der Kultur,* the sickness of my

I and why I write letters like this?

I am not who I think I am, says my guru Blake in the psychodrama of his *Prophecies,* I am why I keep writing.

One Saturday afternoon around ten years ago I was reading The New York Times film reviews in the library, and a very cute child happened to sit opposite me at the little table.

Then as he whispered to himself the lines in his huge illustrated children's book, his lips were so adorable I rushed for a scrap of paper and drew with my ballpoint a thumbnail masterpiece of him in only a minute before he got up and left.

He was an Asian boy about kindergarten age like a Japanese kid in an Ozu film and by magic I was able to catch his exquisite features with just a few strokes.

It was actually the best drawing I had ever done in my whole life and I wanted to keep it, but no, how could I? I was going to give it to him but wasn't sure what he would make of it, and so spotting an old woman my age sitting nearby, I slipped it to her instead.

Then as I was scanning the shelves of DVD's for my weekly fix of films, she came to me holding the hand of the child who said to me so sweetly that it broke my heart:

"Can I have another one to give to my mother?"

"I'm so sorry I can't," I said," but you can make a Xerox of it and give it to her."

He probably didn't know what a Xerox was nor would his immigrant grandmother, but there was nothing else I could do, and I left in a daze.

The whole episode happened in a flash like a dream, but it was one of the highlights of my life, since that little boy was the grandchild I never had, and in my revelation I neglected to even ask his name.

Armenia, 7 December 1988

The following is about when I was a Fulbright Lecturer at the University of Armenia in Yerevan when it was still part of the Soviet Union. I lived in a dorm for foreign lecturers and graduate students, and in the meantime I painted with the art students in the Art Institute around the corner whom I joined in the volunteer rescue trip to the city of what was then called Leninakan that had been hit by the earthquake.

Foreigners weren't allowed there at first, but Gago snuck me into the bus.

"He's one of us," he told the official in charge. *"Hye-ga-gan-eh.* He's Armenian."

And so, we rode into the highland along the mountains, our bus loaded with supplies.

"You're finally getting to see the countryside," Gago said sitting next to me by the window, his deep eyes and craggy nose like the land itself. *"Absos* , alas, it has to be like this."

He was only twenty-eight, yet his face seemed glazed with history as he pointed to the mountains he once climbed with a backpack, the original Armenians a mountain people since pre-history.

Yura, sitting across the aisle, pointed to where his parents still lived.

"Yura's a country bumpkin," Gago joked, and Yura agreed with a big smile.

They were all young enough to be my sons, and yet men at the height of their strength and quickness.

"I'm hungry," Khatchig said, and he started ripping the bread and sausage.

Outside the window the quiet landscape seemed to lie like the giant body of Poseidon the Earth-shaker now resting peacefully after he had killed and maimed while our bus crawled the hills like an ant to a shattered hive.

It was dusk when we arrived and the broken city was dusted pink in the winter haze, the streets clogged with cars and trucks as we walked from the outskirts into a frenzy of men rushing like ants that had lost their lines, the others waiting to dig or pass the buckets of dust and stones.

Then it was dark and cold when we walked to an open space that had been a park, and leaving our supplies on the ground we searched for work at one of the mounds that must have been a high-rise.

The only light was a single beam from one of the tractors in the street, and the noise of its motor kept grinding in counterpoint to the cacophony of the yelling while its beam focused on the mound like a spotlight for a movie set.

More than a day had passed since the quake, but the government relief had been slow to arrive from the other soviets, and the swarms of Armenians were of little use without equipment, yet we joined them in passing the buckets back and forth.

Household buckets and toy buckets and too many of us to be able to move as we shivered in the cold. We would have been warmer digging with our hands, and the dust choked us wherever we stood.

We worked or tried to for several hours, but we were too many for the few spots, and we finally just watched. No bodies had been uncovered, and as we stood on the mound the dust seeped into our lungs as if it were the dead themselves.

Exhausted and cold, we returned to our camp in what had been a park in the square of the buildings, and the families who had escaped were squatting around little fires like the one we started with scrap-wood from the rubble.

Gago, not wanting to stop working, went with Khatchig to roam the dark streets, and the rest of us huddled around our fire while turning our faces from the smoke when the wind changed.

About an hour later a truck arrived with bread and bottled water, and then Khatchig and Gago returned and said they had found a site where we might be helpful at the break of dawn.

Waiting until then, we stared at the flames and rubbed our hands from the cold and smoked cigarettes like hobos, Yura and some others diverting the horror with sex jokes I couldn't understand with my remedial Armenian and limited vocabulary.

In the cold darkness the horror turned the other fires of the families into a moving scene as if they were glowing figures of a powerful drama, and in their shadows they made me think of the refugees in the memoirs of the death march while the night seemed to cowl them like an eternal audience of suffering.

Sleepless and weary, the hours passed with the sex jokes and the bottles of the homemade mulberry whiskey that some of the boys had brought with the supplies, and then as they dozed I stared at the dying embers in the flames.

It was the hour of the dogwatch most prized by monks for deepest meditation, and as I stared at the embers I remembered the same hour in the Japanese monastery in Bodh Gaya while the drone of the tractor by the men digging in the mound mixed with the dying embers of the fire growing more and more beautiful, and I remembered the roshi of the monastery leading the way to a basement where we would continue to sit on our zafus facing the walls until dawn.

So too did I now dig in the mound of my memory as in the monastery when the basement had felt like a tomb until the roshi led the way up the steps for the chanting, and the drone of the tractor was now like that chanting and the red of the embers was like the dawn that was breaking when our chanting grew louder and louder, until one of the monks stood up and walked outside to a long log by a huge bell while our chanting climaxed at the very moment he swung the log into the bell and the huge gong resounded over the little Bodh-gaya like a giant herald of the sun, its long rays streaming into the monastery like an illumination.

Such was that dawn in Bodh Gaya where the Buddha was awakened, but no rays were streaming now and no bell gonged over the rooftops.

Instead there was just the drone of the tractor as the sparrows chirped away the darkness into the nacred light of the morning haze and the mound appeared across the street like a naked skull.

Then the square came into view with the different families exposed to the sky and a statue of Lenin was rising above them with his fist in the air pointing to the mound.

"The statue of Lenin is still standing," I said to Gago.

"Of course," he said, scratching himself awake, "they made sure those statues were built to last, unlike the buildings."

And he lit another cigarette and left it in his lips as he rubbed his hands over the embers. He must have smoked almost a pack since leaving Yerevan.

"Eat something," I said, as if I were his father. "How are you going to work if you smoke instead of eating?"

"I'm not hungry," he said, "the tea will be enough."

Then Khatchig led the way through the quiet streets with the broken glass crackling under our feet and some jars were still stacked in a shop on a corner as if we were walking through Pompeii or an abandoned movie set.

"Remember the streets," Gago said, "so you can return to the square in case we get separated; can you read the signs?"

"No," I said, "I never learned the script, but I'll remember the way."

And like Michelangelo's figure gazing at the skull of Death at the bottom of Hell in *The Last Judgment*, I felt more amazed than horrified, as if I were in a dream where no harm could come to me while everyone else was dead.

I had no family or friends in Leninakan and I felt more alien than ever before from the rest of human kind, as if I were so cold blooded I couldn't feel anything for them, and yet the broken dreamlike city had become more real than any in my waking life, and in the adrenalin speed and hypnotic spell of no sleep, I rushed as if to catch a performance in a theatre.

It was in another mound by a square, only smaller than the one by our camp, and it had been a natal hospital, and the digging was even quicker after a baby was rescued during the night.

But the dead lay covered by sheets at the side of the square, and the long-faced families sat near them waiting and hoping for another miracle.

The dust of the mound felt familiar by now, and we plunged into the digging as if we had been doing it all our lives, tying and untying the cables around the concrete slabs as the giant crane

lifted and lowered them by the corpses like a mythical crane
with a bundled baby dangling from its beak.

And so, we stood in the mound of the little stones of the
broken concrete that was pink and grey from the tufa typical of
Armenian buildings, and the dust continued to fill our lungs as we
hauled away what remained of its architecture and engineering.

And in the fragments of the floors and the twisted skeleton
of their steel emerged the shredded cloth and splintered furniture and rolls of gauze and syringes and little plastic toys and
dolls, so many little plastic toys and dolls that were the most
horrifying of all.

But where were the bodies, there should have been more
than the dozen under sheets in the courtyard? Were they in the
dust, were they in our lungs? Later I would learn that only hair
remained when such a weight came crushing down.

I want to feel a body, said the part of me like Monet study-
ing the light on the cadaver of his beloved wife, as if I could feel
death and taste it and know it: *I want to see someone in all these
stones and dust.*

Maybe there was another baby buried alive, yet we were
really digging for the dead, and their sheets and coffins would
appear everywhere in the next few days.

And so, we shoveled and hauled all morning, but no body
emerged, and by noon there was less to do after more men had
arrived.

"Comon," Gago said, "Vartan found some homes nearby
where we can be more useful."

Delirious with fatigue and the amazing horror, I followed
him and Vartan through the unreal city as if on an acid trip
where everywhere lay bright in the noon sun like a lightning
crack between the living and the dead, the crackle of glass
beneath our shoes the only sound in the ghostly quiet.

Then suddenly Souren was waving from up the street, and
we met him halfway.

"Petros!" he moaned, and though his face was familiar from
the institute where I had painted with him, he was not the same
Souren.

He had not been on the bus but had come on his own. He was from Leninakan and back in the institute he had wanted me to see it.

"I wanted to show you my lovely Leninakan," he said. "Now look at it."

He was on his way to his home that was only cracked. His family was unharmed and he was helping them to leave, and as he talked in the empty street it became not only his childhood but like my own, and we looked at each other as if to confirm we were still alive while our childhood memories were like the rubble and the broken glass.

"Come," Vartan said, "we have work to do."

A few blocks further we came to a narrow street with four-story homes like where I grew up in West Hoboken when each home had a different story and I would peek through doors to see who lived inside, but the collapse of the roofs had become like the wobbly lines in my childhood drawings and everyone was gone.

A few men were working on one of them, and some families sat on the sidewalk looking up as they waited like those at the natal hospital.

Yet the rubble here felt more intimate than in the mounds, intimate from *intimare,* to hint, as in a secret, and by now the dust I breathed felt as part of me as my blood and bones.

A man seemed to know where to dig, and helping him tear away the shreds of lathing and plaster, I felt embarrassed in retrieving the remnants of a kitchen or a bedroom as if I were invading their privacy.

But the man worked nonstop, and in trying to keep up with him I fell faint from fatigue, and I had to climb down to the street where a woman gave me a bottle of water to clear my throat.

Then digging again, I continued to find the different relics in the dust as if from a buried civilization, and I laid aside for the garbage or recycling pile the shards of dishes and splinters of furniture and the dusty clothes and toys and more toys and fragments of who knew what, and still no body or face.

Then the man wanted me to focus on a certain spot, and I

hurried to dig and pull away the scraps of plaster and lathing, until I was on my knees stretching into a jagged hole as if into a secret hideaway.

Then suddenly there appeared the hem of a dress and then a knee and a bicep.

"Oh!" the man cried, looking over my shoulder.

"Oh!" he kept crying, and he turned away with his face in his hands.

She must have been about eleven or twelve, and her leg emerged from the dust with an intimacy only the dead can offer.

Touch her, said somewhere inside me, *touch her leg and uncover her face.*

"Come away!" Gago yelled, and he pulled at me not to look because he himself didn't want to look.

Let me dig! I wanted to say. *I need to see her face! I need to see her face!*

"Come!" Gago kept saying, and he pulled me away as if to pull himself away.

"Our work here is done."

No! I wanted to say. *I need to see her face! I need to see her face!*

And I kept scraping away the plaster and the lathing, but her torso was buried under a beam and it would take hours to pull her out.

And when I touched her leg I felt ashamed, as if she were more alive than ever before, and feeling its coldness I wanted to keep touching as if my touching could revive her.

"Help me pull her out!" I said to Gago.

"No," he said, horrified. "There will be others for that."

He had friends in Leninikan and she could have been one of them. She had been the niece of the man who was now crying on the other side of the rubble, and she had a face and a name.

Who was she? Why did I need to touch her, why did I need to see her face, as if she were the visionary girl in my pubescent dream whom I would never forget.

But unable to say this to Gago, I let him pull me away, and we climbed down to the street.

I should have stayed, I kept thinking, I should have uncovered her face.

Back in the camp there was food from a supply truck, and Yura was roasting potatoes in the fire, his face alive and bright and the potatoes delicious in their charred skin, the bottled water soothing my throat that was parched from all the cigarettes and dust, everyone vibrant and more alive than ever before in the middle of the dead.

The foreign help was arriving after the Soviet delays and more men appeared until there was a surplus of diggers and we weren't needed anymore, yet we didn't want to leave though we had no ground cloths or sleeping bags, but unable to endure another sleepless night we returned to Yerevan to rest.

Back at the dorm my room was the same as before, yet it no longer seemed solid, and when I bathed in the little tub the dust flowed into the drain and the drain led to the same kind of pipes and walls where I had dug, and the soap and the mirror seemed to float in a phenomena that would also crumble into another mound someday.

Then lying in my bed in the darkness I kept seeing the leg of the girl emerging from the dust, and I would feel its coldness for the rest of my life.

But in the morning my doves were waiting for the breadcrumbs and wheat berries I had been feeding them on the windowsill, and their copper and violet colors were more beautiful than ever in the winter light, the glimmering ebony of their innocent eyes like the girl herself and the buildings in the distance in cubes of pink and blue like a peaceful Cezanne with a buried torso in montage.

And so, we rode in another bus back to Leninakan, and we were in our camp by evening, as if we had come home again.

There were wooden coffins everywhere by now, and they reminded us that this was still a city and not yet a Pompeii or the Forum in Rome.

Searching again for where we could be useful, we walked
behind Khatchig's searchlight, and the dark streets were so
peaceful and intimate they felt like my childhood fantasy of
wandering anywhere I wanted as if there were no private property any more.

And we came to a huge mound as wide as a football field
that must had been a complex of apartment buildings where
dozens of men were digging wherever the lights could reach
them in the sea of dust and rubble.

And at one spot I dug into what must have been a large
closet, and reaching into it I pulled away a pile of coats that
must have belonged to a wealthy woman who had a taste for
fur and Persian lamb, and each one emerged from the hole like
a rabbit from a magician's derby: coat after coat but no flesh or
bone, until they lay in a pile like pelts that were still alive.

Then Gago reached into the rubble behind me, and he
retrieved a little book with a title in Cyrillic that I couldn't read.

"It's by Hegel," he said, thumbing through the pages. "It's
Hegel's *Philosophy of History.*"

"Have you ever read Hegel?" I said.

"No," he said, "we were supposed to in school because of
Marx, but I never did. Have you ever read Hegel?"

"No, I never did either."

"Well," he said, "whoever did won't need him anymore."

And he flipped it back into the rubble as if it were the only
reality, his young beard dusted grey in the bluish light like Dante
standing on the mound of the dead.

"What are you doing?" he said. "Why are you putting that
stone in your pocket?"

"It's a *hishadag,*" I said, a souvenir. "I always take a stone
from somewhere important, ever since I was a kid."

"You want a souvenir of death?" he said.

"I don't know of what," I said.

"Let's get back to work," he said, "we're not here for
souvenirs."

We slept for a few hours in the bus that night, and the driver
had kept the heater on as we curled into each other in the double

seats, as if we were travelling somewhere.

We slept only two hours, but it was enough, and then it was dawn and we looked for work again.

It was Sunday, four days after the quake. Survivors seemed unlikely by now, but news of success increased our strength, and we walked to another part of the city.

"Look!" Yura said, pointing to a big yellow crane, "the Japanese have come."

Then we came to two Swiss volunteers talking German to a local interpreter, and everyone stood back so the dogs could sniff in the mounds.

They were big beautiful shepherds that panted and sniffed for the odor of life, and we stood admiring their animal magic, but their barking was not the kind that was needed.

"They're very tired," said the Swiss volunteer in German. "They've been held up in Moscow all night and they had no sleep."

Then we wandered to another district where the mound had been a primary school, and a dozen coffins lay on the street near a supply of gas masks, but the masks were unused because the bodies were frozen and the odor still faint.

It was a sweet sick odor like skunk, and it lingered over the coffins in the frosty air.

We tried to work and then just sat on the side drinking tea and smoking cigarettes with the other workers, while the coffins lay only a few yards away.

One worker was a jolly old Armenian peasant who wanted to hear stories about America, and his smile seemed to say there was no shame in feeling friendly in the middle of death. He had come to work and was now resting and drinking tea.

"Do they have quakes this big in America?" he asked.

I wanted to stay another night, but I had a very bad cold by now, and Gago pushed me to a bus returning to Yerevan with some workers from a wine-making collective in the south.

Then back at the dorm old Khosrof, the evening clerk, was sitting at his desk in his huge grey overcoat and furry astrakhan with the flaps down, his raccoon eyes peering over the counter and his deep voice rasping like a bullfrog from the underworld of his cigarette lungs.

He was an old vet who had survived the Stalin years and was now supplementing his pension by sitting here like a furry witness to the in and out of life.

"You have a message from Stella," he said.

Stella had finally found a ride to Leninakan as an interpreter, and she had taken a call for me before she left.

"Harry Smith," she wrote, "wants to talk with you. He's from CBS and he will call again tomorrow. The phones are so bad he will have to keep trying."

He must have located me through the State Department and my Fulbright.

My cold turned into a fever, but it was gone after a long sleep, and the next morning, feeling drugged by my body's cure against the virus, I walked down to the lobby and sat by the heater with old Hripsimeh, the day clerk in charge of the good phone that she would keep clear in case Harry Smith got through.

Some of the students in the dorm were playing ping-pong while others yelled into the bad phone trying to be heard, old Guyana cooking *tanaboor* in the buffet while Ararat the commandant watched the news with his cronies in his office, each of them knowing someone who died.

Then the mail arrived and there was a telegram from my friend Bob Hass back in Berkeley.

"Pete," it said, *"are you all right?"* It must have cost him more than twenty bucks, which was a lot in those days, and I would always remember this.

Then Mufid came in from the cold and he shook his pink and chubby cheeks. He was a graduate student in mathematics from Syria.

"Is terrible," he said in English. "You see it?"

"Yes, I saw it."

"Is terrible, no?"

"Yes, it was terrible."

"Terrible," he said, the *b* delicious on his Arabic tongue, his beautiful Arab eyes expressive and bright.

"Come," Hripsimeh said in Armenian. "Come eat *tanaboor* with me."

And laying the bowls on the desk with the *tutvatz* of pickled cabbage, she unfolded the big sheets of the fresh flatbread that was not sold in the shops but baked by someone she knew around the corner.

She was bundled up in several layers of sweaters and socks, and her old face was like my mother's inside the scarf around her neck, a few teeth missing in her smile.

Like old Khosrof she was retired from working in a factory, but she originally came from a peasant village and grew up with flatbread she once baked herself by slapping the dough on the sides of a hole in the ground.

She tore it apart and stuffed it with a soft cheese the same as my mother would make, and she chewed it with her side teeth as she slurped the *tanaboor.*

It was cooked with barley like the wheat-berries I fed my doves on my windowsill, and it was sprinkled with dried mint like my mother's. It was a good hot soup made with yoghurt and I had been eating it since I was a child, and the *tutvatz* made it even more delicious.

Then the phone finally rang, and the voice of a Harry Smith came through the static and the odors of the yoghurt and vinegar.

He was a newsmonger who gathered suffering and sold it like produce for dinnertime. People on the other side of the world watched it on television instead of eating in silence, and should I who had been one of them say no?

No, you can't have this suffering; I don't want it to contribute to your million dollar salary.

Instead another part of me talked with him as if the world would care, even at the price of making me a fool.

"Listen," Harry Smith said with the smoothness of his trade, "this is going to be transmitted live and I want you to tell us your personal feelings."

"My personal feelings in three minutes?"

"Well, do the best you can," he said.

And so, I talked to Harry Smith while Hripsimeh looked up and listened to my English that she couldn't understand.

"What did you tell him?" she said afterwards.

"I can't remember," I said.

Months later my brother's wife would tell me she heard my voice on her little kitchen television while she was chopping vegetables for dinner.

I continued to rest in the dorm until Stella returned. She had interpreted for a group of English firemen, and they had rescued a little girl who had been buried alive in one of the mounds.

She had talked to the girl looking into a hole and comforting her while the firemen dug her out. She was very tired now, but her face was bright with the rescue, and then she paused and looked out the window as she remembered one of the mounds.

A family had wanted to know about the bodies of their relatives, and she had translated the question to one of the firemen.

"The fireman told me," she said gravely, "that when a building that big comes down, all that's left of a body is hair. Now how was I supposed to translate that?"

By midweek my cold lingered in its peaceful phase of slow motion and a husky voice. But where was Svetya? She was late again.

When she finally came her foot was bruised from a fall while running back home for the identification card she had forgotten and needed to show old Khosrof before he would allow her upstairs, and she limped through the lobby that was full of young Russian volunteers who had been sleeping on the floor.

"I'm sorry I'm late," she said.

"That's okay," I said, "I'm more than happy to see you."

One of the common rooms on the second floor was packed with leftovers from the American relief teams, and stacks of toilet paper were among the cans of macaroni and beans that were left for the refugees.

Asking for some rolls would have been embarrassing and I would get some from Gunter who taught German at the university and would be hitching a flight to West Germany with the

German relief team. He would also return with toothpaste and condoms that would remind me of my easy life in the west.

Yet how expensive Svetya would have been back there, and I would never be able to afford anyone like her again.

She had drunk some *"champagnski "* and was turned on, but I couldn't make her come. She squirmed and stretched and crawled all over me, until she finally said:

"I can't, you don't have to try anymore. Come, you make yourself happy."

After so much death my hunger for her felt even more intense, as if this were the last time it would be gratified.

Then in the pulse of the quiet she asked about my little stone souvenir that was glowing under the lamplight, its delicate roughness like a work of art in a museum.

Did she know anyone in Leninakan? I asked. Of course, she said, everyone knew someone from Leninikan, but she didn't want to talk about whoever they were.

The warmth of her flesh felt more alive than ever before, and the little vein in her neck was like a lifeline of her sweetness, the silence of the room pulsing with the memory of the mounds and nothing left but hair, her long black hair luxuriant in the lamplight like a gift from the deep.

Juju

And now she nuzzles in my arm with her belly on my crotch, my left hand holding her and my right writing this. And I want to write more of her, of her life in the backyard and how she flaps through her door and meows hello, of how she likes to sleep on my clothes as if she loves the smell of me, my substitute wife and family whose warmth warms me as mine does her. But I have to piss now after drinking two bottles of Bass Ale feeling lonely, yet I don't want to let go of her; she feels so good I want to keep holding her and writing this; O Loneliness, thank you for leading me here....And now, Sweetie, I really do need to piss, or is it that I don't know what else to write, nor take more pleasure before wanting something else. What else is there? A shower and then sleep and then another day of being human while you will be a cat....And she rises and jumps off, as if she's telepathic, like when she's in the yard and yet knows the moment I wake in the morning; then she flaps through the hole in the door and sits Egyptian style with her forelegs straight, as if to say I should feed her, the killer of beautiful birds, herself beautiful. And I do.

Monday, ten p.m. 6 December 1999

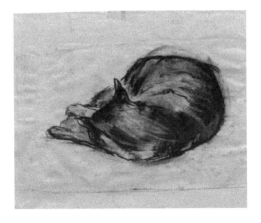

Acknowledgments

In abiding gatitude to all who pre-paid for copies to have this book published:

John Ruhlman, Bobby Ohannesian, Lenny Silverberg, Dobby and Judy Boe, Henry Bean, Atom Egoyan, Bob Hass, Bob Maniquis, Luke Hass, Susan Chasson, Carmela Cohen, Giorgia Neidorf, Marian Hjortsberg, Judith Thomas, Manda Heron, Ann Martin, Helen Van Gelder, Nancy Kricorian, Aris Janigian, Francesco Rosato and Ayako Harashima, Peter Nagourney, Tory Topjian, Gwen Mazoujian, Norik Khachikians, Beate Hepke, Roupen and Zovig Donikian, Ron Samarian, Randy Hughes, Paul Moore, Ron Kane, Ruth Pizer, Bobby Berg, Bob Houghteling, Dennis Osmond, Michael Darby, Victor Ichioka, Witt Monts, Denny Negrini, Johnny Massaro, Mimi Malayan, Samuela Evans, Mary Kandalian, Armen and Nelly Der Kiureghian, Alvart Badalian, Stephanie's Art Gallery, Arpi Sarafian, Lilit Kazangyan, Hrag Varjabedian, Lisa Greenstein, Nathaniel Ruhlman, Ethan Maniquis, Tim Spaulding, Anthony DeCicco, Jon Stewart, Richard Goulian, Jeanie Amerkanian, Ruel Bernard, Roxanne Makasdjian, Blake Maniquis, and Michelle Cohen, Pamina Taylor, Melissa Martin, John Montoya, Karina Epperlein, Joan Alexander, Clive Matson.

Thank you, Bob Hass, for sending *The Minor Third* to Michael Ondaatje who got it published in Brick Magazine and for sending *The Dead* to Wendy Lesser who put it in her Threepenny Review. Thank you, Charles Entrekin for publishing *Yellow* and *The No Money Work* in your on-line magazine, Sisyphus. Thank you, Aris Janigian, for publishing *Freud's Story* and *After The Massacre* in your on-line magazine, The Artifactuals. Thank you Todd Kerr for publishing *Juju* in your Berkeley Times.

*The author's quick ball point sketch of publisher Mark Weiman
at the computer while feeding the scanner with the last of the
illustrations for this book. May 25, 2021*

ON OTHER BOOKS BY THE AUTHOR:

"Holds the reader captivated." On *Voyages*, NY Times Book Review, 1971.

"It lingers in the mind." William Saroyan on *Voyages*, in a note to Pantheon Books, 1971.

"Perfect!" On *Wash me On Home*, Mama, American Book Review, 1978.

"A magical book." On *Daughters of Memory*, NY Times Book Review,1986.

". . . A daring book nearer in feeling to Whitman's *Out of the Cradle Endlessly Rocking* or Ginsberg's *Kaddish* than to any wortk of prose I can think of." Robert Hass on *Daughter's of Memory*, 1986.

"A remarkable work." On *The Great American Loneliness*, Choice Review, 1998.

"I hope it will find the warm and wide reception it deserves." Michael Arlen on *The Great American Loneliness,* 1998.

"Filled with a joyful, comic light." Leo Litwak on *The Great American Loneliness,* 1998.

"I was deeply impressed and moved." Hank Heifetz on *The Artist and His Mother,* 2010.

"His voice is unique in American letters." Dickran Kyoumjian on *The Artist and His Mother,* , 2010.

"It's very beautiful." Henry Bean on *The Artist and His Mother,* 2010.

"Najarian's own paintings capture stunning visions of motifs in San Francisco Bay Area locations, which are among the finest plein air depictions of California in recent times." Terry St. John on *The Paintings of Art Pinajian, 2015*

"As for art—it also matters that Najarian is a remarkable painter which makes *The Naked and The Nude* as much about seeing and making as it is a book about sexuality. The intensely vivid paintings and drawings reproduced here are reason enough to have the book on your shelf." Robert Hass on *The Naked and The Nude,* 2017.

CPSIA information can be obtained
at www.ICGtesting.com
Printed in the USA
LVHW021110010721
691612LV00003B/7

9 781587 906039